HOT MESS

A *HOSTILE OPERATIONS TEAM* Novella

USA TODAY BESTSELLING AUTHOR

LYNN RAYE HARRIS

Copyright ©2013 by Lynn Raye Harris
Cover Design Copyright © 2013 Croco Designs
Formatting by JT Formatting

www.**lynnrayeharris**.com

Printed in the United States of America

First Edition: November 2013
Library of Congress Cataloging-in-Publication Data

Harris, Lynn Raye
    Hot Mess: A Hostile Operations Team Novella / 1st ed

    ISBN-13: 978-0-9894512-9-1

    1.   Hot Mess—Fiction. 2. Fiction—Romance
    3.   Fiction—Contemporary Romance

DEDICATION

To my readers! Y'all rock! Thanks for embracing the men of HOT and the women who tame them.

PROLOGUE

Hopeful, Texas

TEXAS SUMMERS MELTED ALL THE good sense a man possessed. That was the only explanation for why Sam McKnight had taken Georgeanne Hayes and driven up toward Hopeful Lake. He hadn't intended to do it at all, but since he'd gotten back home on leave from the Army three days ago, he'd noticed one thing in this town that had changed dramatically: Georgie Hayes.

"You home for long?" Georgie asked.

He turned the car—an old truck he'd borrowed from his mother—onto the dirt track that ran around the south side of the lake. It was nearly dark now, the sun a glimmer of a memory on the horizon.

"Just a few days."

"I've missed you, Sam."

He shot her a grin. "I missed you too. Your whole family," he added. The Hayes family had always been more of a family to him than his own. Her brother was his best friend in the world—which meant he should *not* be thinking of Georgie as anything more than the annoying little kid she'd always been. She used to follow him around whenever he was at her house, her barely concealed crush almost embarrassing to witness. He'd ignored it, which hadn't been difficult to do when she'd been twelve and he fifteen.

But now she was eighteen—and impossible to ignore.

He could feel her pouting in the silence that followed. God she'd changed. In ways he still couldn't wrap his head around.

"I was hoping maybe you'd missed me the most," she said softly.

"If I'd known you'd turn out like this, I might have." *Shut up, Sam.*

Because he knew, as sure as he knew his own name, that he was *not* what Richard Hayes Sr. had in mind for his little princess. Georgie was going to the University of Texas, where she'd study something suitably refined—interior design, perhaps—and marry the star quarterback.

He was just a soldier home on leave—and he had nothing to offer besides a healthy libido and a few stolen nights of passion.

"It was inevitable. Mama was Miss Dallas, you know."

Yeah, he knew. But that didn't mean he'd ever thought of Georgie as anything more than Rick's little sister. Yet here she was, with curves in all the right places, an impressive rack, and the most gorgeous chocolate-brown hair that tumbled in waves over her shoulders and fell all the way to her ass.

He found a place to park and turned off the engine. His heart pounded in his chest as he turned to look at her.

What the hell was he doing again? He needed to drive straight back to town and forget every dirty thought he'd been thinking about her since she'd walked into the bowling alley an hour ago.

She gazed at him with eyes that he felt like he could drown in. Green eyes, like springtime in the country.

"I'm eighteen now."

"I know."

She slicked her tongue over pretty pink lips. "Then maybe you'll finally kiss me."

He could only stare at her for a long moment, his brain warring with his dick. She was still his best friend's baby sister, and he had a duty to protect her just the same as Rick would if he were here. Sam had driven her out here, but only because she'd asked him to.

Dumbass. You know exactly why she asked, and you also know why you did it.

"I'm not sure it's a good idea, Georgie."

She unclipped her seatbelt and moved toward him. "I am. I want to kiss you, Sam. Hell, I want you. I've wanted you since I was thirteen."

He swallowed hard. His voice, when he spoke, was hoarse. "You don't mean that."

She slid up close and put her arms around his neck. "Like hell I don't. Oh, I didn't know what I wanted at thirteen. But I do now. I want *you*, Sam. I want you to fuck me."

"Christ, Georgie, don't talk like that." His hands spanned her ribcage. He intended to set her away from him, but somehow he wasn't managing it.

And Georgie knew it.

"Why not? Does it turn you on?"

Did it turn him on? Shit, he was harder than an ice cube in Siberia. "I'm not here to stay. You know that, right? I gotta leave in two days and go back to the Army."

"I know."

"You asked me if I was home for long."

She sighed. "Small talk, Sam. I know you aren't staying. But I want you anyway."

He shouldn't do it. He knew he shouldn't. He should start the truck and drive back toward town. But he wasn't going to. He was weak and, from the moment she'd walked up to him looking like this, he was lost. With a groan, Sam lowered his mouth to hers and kissed her.

ONE

Twelve years later…

"I'M SORRY, DR. HAYES, BUT we can't give out that kind of information."

Georgeanne gritted her teeth in frustration. She'd been getting the same answer for two days now. Military bureaucracy at its finest. She gripped the phone and tried to keep her voice calm. "Sergeant Hamilton has not formally withdrawn, but he's not been to class for the last three sessions. Surely you know if he's been deployed."

The woman on the other end didn't miss a beat. "I'm not allowed to give out that information, Dr. Hayes. We don't discuss our personnel with unauthorized persons."

Georgeanne sighed and pressed her hand to her forehead. "Fine. Can someone just submit a withdrawal form on his behalf? It will save him getting an F, which will affect his GPA."

And if she knew anything about Jake Hamilton, she knew for a fact he didn't want that. He was dead-set on graduating with honors and applying for Officer Training

School. If it came down to it, she'd submit the form herself. It was against policy, but she'd argue for an exception in this case.

"I'll see what we can do."

After the niceties were finished, Georgeanne hung up the phone and suppressed the urge to scream. If she were at home alone, in her little Alexandria townhouse, she might do just that. But she was currently sitting in a coffee shop in the Pentagon concourse, waiting for her class to start.

The military did a fine job of encouraging its members to go to school, gave them plenty of money for tuition, and provided space on military installations around the world for universities to teach classes and offer degree programs. The only issue for most of her students was time, since they also had very demanding jobs.

Which was where her concern for Sergeant Hamilton had come in. This was the third course he'd taken with her, and she'd never known him to miss a single session without first informing her of any temporary duty he might have. Not that he couldn't have had an emergency, but when he missed the third class in a row, she'd begun to wonder. It just wasn't like him to be irresponsible.

If he didn't show up tonight, it would be the fourth time. Two weeks of class was a lot in an eight-week term. Not only that, but finals were next week, and if he didn't come tonight, he'd never be prepared. She'd e-mailed him a couple of times now, and she'd even called the number he'd put on the information sheet she collected from every student at the beginning of the term.

There had been no reply to her calls or her e-mails, which seemed very odd.

Georgeanne frowned over her coffee. Jake had often come early to class and joined her here for something to drink. She had an open door policy for students and, while he hadn't needed much help with assignments, he seemed to like to talk to her about the books they read. Since she enjoyed teaching literature, she welcomed the rare student who got really excited about the material.

The last time she'd seen Jake, he'd been sitting on a bench in the Pentagon Metro. She'd walked over to talk to him before the train arrived. He'd seemed a bit preoccupied, but she hadn't thought too much about it since her students were adults with busy lives.

When the train came, he did not get on. He'd told her he was waiting for a friend so they could go out to a bar in Crystal City. The last Georgeanne had seen of him, he'd been talking to a dark-haired man with a manicured beard. Georgeanne had waved again as the train pulled out. The man standing with Jake turned, his hard gaze meeting hers. He'd looked angry, threatening in a way that shocked her. She'd snatched her hand into her lap and turned her head, breaking eye contact.

And then she'd been angry with herself for reacting that way. She was a grown woman, independent, and she didn't like that a man had made her feel unsafe just by looking at her angrily.

But then she'd gone home, taken a hot bath, immersed herself in a book, and forgotten about Jake and his friend.

Now Georgeanne checked the time on her phone, and then she gathered her computer and purse and made her way down to the basement where her class was being held. Two and a half hours later, she retraced her path through the Pentagon and down to the Metro station that lay beneath the building.

Jake had not come to class, but then she hadn't really expected him to. As she stood in the station with the hot air blowing through the tunnels and ruffling her hair, she decided that tomorrow she was calling that woman at his unit and trying again.

She knew she should just leave well enough alone, knew that the military did what they wanted when they wanted. Though they could have shipped him off in the middle of the night for some sort of duty, he wasn't in the Special Forces. He worked in a general's office as a low-level administrative assistant. Not typically the kind of guy to disappear without notice.

Georgeanne yawned and stepped forward as the rush of air intensified ahead of the next train. She was so ready to take a hot bath and climb into bed with a good book and her cat. The sad state of her life these days, she supposed.

A bright light shone from the tunnel as the train fast approached. The station wasn't crowded at this time of night, but as Georgeanne waited on the platform, someone jostled her. Hard. It was so surprising that she didn't realize at first what was happening. It was as if she were tipping forward in slow motion. It took a moment to realize she was falling.

Georgeanne screamed as the darkness below the platform yawned up at her.

Staff Sergeant Sam McKnight stood in front of a townhouse on a shaded Alexandria street and took a deep breath. It was early morning and the sun was shining bright. The sky already had that hazy look that meant they were in for another humid day in the DC Metro area. It was hotter than blazes, but not quite as hot as Texas. Or as hot as where he'd just returned from.

Texas might be hot, but the Arabian Desert was hotter. He could say that for a fact now. He looked down at his uniform—crisp BDUs—and wondered if he should have saved this visit for another time, when he could show up in jeans and a T-shirt and look halfway like the guy Georgie would remember.

But he'd just gotten back to the States recently and he was looking forward to seeing an old friend—at least he hoped Georgie was still his friend. He hadn't known she was in DC until he'd called Rick just a few days ago.

"Could you check on her for me, man?" Rick asked. "I think the divorce messed with her head. She seems sad. Won't come home to Texas, insists on staying in DC and teaching college classes."

Sam frowned. He had no idea what kind of reception Georgie might give him. He hadn't seen her since she'd married Tim Cash six years ago. Before that, the last time he'd seen her was when she'd been naked in the front seat of his truck and he'd nearly taken everything she'd offered. He'd had the good sense to stop, but he wasn't sure she'd ever forgiven him for it.

"Sure. But you're her brother. Why don't you just call her and ask how she is?"

Rick blew out a breath. "I call her every week, but she never says anything. She avoids my questions about

9

time at her house as a kid, her expression changed into something that looked too much like pity for comfort. "Oh, Sam, I didn't mean—"

He stood abruptly. The one thing he couldn't stomach from anyone was pity. "I have to get to work, Georgie. I just wanted to stop by and see how you were."

She looked up at him, her eyes bright. He hoped those weren't tears. If they were, he was sunk. Georgie Hayes crying always brought out his protective instincts. She bit her lip and looked away again. "Of course. But can I ask you something first?"

A wave of tension rolled through him. He had no idea what the fuck she might ask. But he couldn't refuse her when it seemed such an easy thing on the surface. "Anything, G. You can ask me anything."

TWO

GEORGEANNE COULDN'T BELIEVE THAT SAM McKnight was standing in her house, looking so damn handsome and perfect and remote that she wanted to scream. When she'd been thirteen, he'd been everything she'd ever wanted in a boy. Three years older than she, he hadn't been interested in the least. But he'd given her a lot of angsty nights dreaming about him.

He'd spent a lot of time at the Hayes' house. His parents didn't have much money, and they all lived in a run-down trailer in the middle of a field about six miles from town. She remembered one summer when Sam had stayed at their house from the day school let out until right before it started again. Her parents hadn't minded. Rick was happy to have his best friend around, and Georgeanne was happy to gaze blissfully at Sam over the dinner table every night.

She remembered when his parents divorced, too. He'd been sixteen, and he'd grown tight-lipped and sullen. He and Rick spent hours playing their guitars and sneaking Dad's beer from the pool house fridge. By then, she'd the guy had to go somewhere for a test."

She'd been working with the military for over a year now, and the acronyms still went over her head sometimes. "DARPA? What's that?"

"It's the Defense Advanced Research Projects Agency. They work on technological projects designed to advance military capabilities around the globe. Real cloak and dagger stuff."

Georgeanne shivered. Jake worked on cloak and dagger projects? "Sounds very secretive."

Sam shrugged. "It is. But what I just told you is the kind of thing you'd find on Wikipedia. The projects are classified, but not the existence of the agency or their basic mission."

Georgeanne frowned as she studied the coffee in her hands. She was being silly. Jake had been sent somewhere, and it was far more important to him than the possibility of a less than perfect GPA. "So he could have just gone away at a moment's notice."

"Very possible."

Yet she couldn't forget that last night in the Metro, when he'd been talking to that man who'd given her a vaguely uneasy feeling. "I guess I can't verify that in any way."

"Probably not." After a moment, Sam sighed, his rigid stance relaxing a hair. "Give me his name and I'll see what I can find out. I'm not promising anything, but maybe if I ask the right people, I can find out when he'll be back at least."

"That would be amazing. Army Sergeant Jake Hamilton."

Sam slapped the beret against his leg. "I really have

to go, G. I have to get out to Maryland before the traffic gets too bad."

Georgeanne dragged herself up, wincing as she put weight on her leg. "I appreciate you checking into this for me."

Sam's expression had turned hard, as if he wanted to punch something. It disconcerted her for a moment, but then she realized it was just his protective instincts coming out. No bully had ever bothered her for long with Sam and Rick around.

"You need to take a hot bath and relax."

She smiled. "Did that last night. I imagine the bruising will only get worse before it gets better."

Sam shoved a hand through his hair, which was sort of senseless since it was cropped so short. It was completely sexy on him. As were the muscles. Georgeanne forced herself to concentrate on his dark, glittering eyes. *Put those muscles from your mind, girl.*

"How did you fall?"

"Someone bumped into me in the Metro. I went down hard." It was the truth, though she left out the part about nearly falling into a train's path. Sam wouldn't hesitate to call Rick about it, and then Rick would call their mother. Cynthia Tolliver Hayes would be on the next plane to DC. Georgeanne suppressed a shudder. She loved her mother, but the woman would suffocate her if she showed up.

Sam took a card from his pocket and wrote a number on it with the pen sitting on her coffee table. His tanned fingers were long and strong, and she found herself shivering involuntarily as she watched him write. Then he straightened again and she tried to force her mind away from his hands.

Hands that had once caressed her so sweetly she'd nearly cried. He'd slid a finger into her wet folds, stroked her until she'd sobbed his name. Her body clenched with the memory, even now. It had been far too long since she'd desired a man, far too long since she'd felt anything remotely like need flare deep inside her.

But, right now, if Sam McKnight asked her to strip naked and lie back on the sofa, she'd do it in a heartbeat.

"Call me if you need anything, Georgie."

She tried not to swallow her tongue. *If she needed anything*. Gawd almighty.

She took the card, and then they stood there awkwardly for several moments while she wondered whether she should give him a friendly hug. How did you hug a man you'd once wanted with every ounce of desire in your body? A man who was currently making you zing with sparks you hadn't felt in a damn long time?

"Goodbye, Georgie."

Her heart turned over, but she managed to smile. "Bye, Sam. It was great seeing you."

"You too." He hesitated so long she thought he might say something else, but then he turned and walked back down the hallway. She listened to the door snick closed behind him, and then she cursed herself up one side and down the other.

Way to go, Georgie-girl.

22

Sam prowled around HOT headquarters like an angry lion. He didn't know why he was so worked up over Georgie needing to know about a soldier. But he was. He could still hear the way she said the guy's name, with such concern, until it twisted up inside his brain and made him want to dig it out by any means possible.

Jake Hamilton. She'd said he was just a good student she was concerned about, but she sounded almost fond of the guy. And that didn't sit quite right with Sam, though God knew he didn't have even the ghost of a reason to care. He'd given up that right a long time ago.

Georgie was off-limits to him. Always had been, even if he'd nearly fucked it up once.

He could still taste her sweet mouth, the nectar of her pussy on his fingers, the drumbeat of hot desire that had pounded in his brain until he'd been nearly mindless with the urge to slide into her body and give them both some sweet relief.

But then she'd whispered that she was still a virgin—that she'd saved herself for him—and he'd known he had to stop. How could he take what she offered with a clear conscience, knowing he could never give her more than a few stolen nights? Georgie had convinced herself she was in love with him when all he wanted was sex. If she'd been anybody else, he might not have cared. But she was Georgie, and he knew he couldn't break her heart like that.

Aside from that one incident, she was like a sister to him. He'd spent long summers at her house, pretending not to notice her following him around like a lovesick puppy, and he'd grown to care about her. Hell, he cared about all the Hayeses. Rick, his mom and dad, and little Georgie. They'd given him shelter when he'd had none, given him a place to be a kid when his house was nothing but a battle-ground.

That was why he'd do whatever he could for any of them. So if Georgie was concerned about Sergeant Hamilton, then Sam would do his best. And he wouldn't feel a pinch in his heart over the way she said the guy's name, or the blatant concern on her face.

He walked back inside the offices where his new squad was located and plopped down at the desk he'd been assigned. There was nothing on it yet but a computer and some binders containing mission briefs.

"Yo, Knight Rider, you got everything you need?"

Sam looked up to find Kevin MacDonald standing over him. Big Mac was the second in command of their squad. No one else was around right now, except Billy "The Kid" Blake, who sat hunched over his computer, fingers flying as he worked to crack some kind of code or write a program. Or, hell, maybe he was hacking into China or something.

Sam had no idea since that wasn't his thing. Weapons, that was his deal. Just give him some guns or explosives, and he was good to go.

It had definitely crossed his mind that the Kid could find Jake Hamilton. If Sam could ever manage to ask him about it. Sam was still new enough that he wasn't quite sure about these guys yet. He'd been training with them pretty hard, and he knew they were all brilliant at what they did. He had no doubt his ass would be safer than all the gold in Fort Knox when he was out on a mission with HOT.

But that didn't mean he felt comfortable enough to ask for information he wanted for personal reasons.

"Yeah, man. Doing great," he answered.

Kev sank into a chair opposite. "So, you go see your friend?"

"Before work." He tapped his fingers on the desk. What the hell. If he didn't at least float the idea, he'd never know. "She teaches college classes at the Pentagon. Says one of her students is missing. An active duty guy."

Kev frowned. "Probably a short notice deployment."

"That's what I told her. She isn't convinced, and no one will give her any information." He leaned back in the seat, bouncing it a little bit. "The guy works for DARPA. Nothing unusual in a short notice assignment."

Kev shrugged. "Ask the Kid. He could locate the record in half a minute. If it's classified, that's the end of it. But maybe he had emergency leave or something. At least then you could tell her not to worry." Kev grinned. "Or maybe you want the guy to stay gone? Give you a chance, right? Is she pretty?"

Sam couldn't find his voice. Was she pretty? Hell yeah. Pretty, and so fucking sexy he could grow hard thinking about her. But he wouldn't. He had too much self-discipline for that.

Keep telling yourself that, ace.

He cleared his throat. "She's like a sister to me, dude. I grew up with her and her brother."

"Ah." Kev stood. "Well then, different story. Hey, Kid, got something for you," he called. Then he winked at Sam and strode out of the room.

Sam glanced over at Billy Blake. The guy was looking at him quizzically. "What you need?"

Georgeanne decided she needed to get out of the house. She had no classes today, but that still wasn't an excuse to lie around and do nothing. Besides, sitting at home, all she could seem to think about was Sam standing in her living room and the mixed up tangle of emotions she'd felt from the moment she opened the door and saw him on her threshold.

It was early on an August day, and the humidity was already approaching unbearable. Still, Georgeanne forged onward until she reached her favorite café, ordered a latte, and took a seat in the corner where she could watch people go by. She'd been there for about a half hour, scrolling through e-mail on her laptop, when a man sat down across from her.

She looked up in surprise. The café wasn't full and there were plenty of other tables. "Hi," he said, smiling broadly. He was dark eyed, dark skinned. His smile did not reach his eyes.

"Can I help you?" She infused her voice with her best frosty tone, learned at the feet of her debutante mother, and waited for him to take the hint.

"You're pretty," he said.

"Thank you, but I'm not interested."

He reached for her hand, gripping it in a surprisingly strong hold. Georgeanne tried to jerk away, but he held her tight. Her heart hammered and her stomach bottomed out as a wave of bitter acid flooded her tongue. She opened her mouth to yell for help.

Before she could say anything, the man leaned forward, his eyes gleaming with malice. "Your lover lied to us, Dr. Hayes. We are not amused. If you don't wish to fall again, you will do what we ask when it is time."

He let her go and shoved back from the table. Georgeanne sat there with her heart in her throat, her skin flushing hot. Her lover? What? She wanted to call out and tell him he had the wrong person, but the man was gone.

And then a river of ice poured down her spine as the rest of his words sank in. Last night hadn't been an accident. Someone had actually *tried* to push her into the path of an oncoming train. Bile rolled in sickening waves in her belly.

Georgeanne sucked in a breath and then another and another as she tried not to hyperventilate. Cold fear gripped her hard, shaking her until her entire body trembled uncontrollably. She darted her gaze around the coffee shop, but no one seemed to be interested in her. Hastily, she grabbed her things and shoved them into her bag with hands that shook so hard she could barely perform the task. She wanted to go home and lock her doors and not come out for a week.

The day was bright, the streets filled with tourists and residents alike. She told herself no one would approach her again as she hurried out to the street. But she walked quickly up the road, though her sore hip ached. She wanted to be inside her house where she could lock the doors and windows, where no stranger could grab onto her like he had the right. Where no one could threaten her.

She reached her street, hurried up her steps and put her key into the lock with trembling fingers. Once inside, she let out a shaky sigh. She set her purse on the table near the door and walked back toward the kitchen and family room. A glass of ice with some vodka and tonic—heavy on the vodka—was just what she needed right about now. Then she could think again.

But when she walked into the kitchen, fear clutched her heart in a cold fist. Her insides liquified. The back door was wide open.

THREE

GEORGEANNE WAS NOT ONE TO fall apart. She'd been raised to be gracious, strong, and flexible in all things. Her mother was pure Texas steel and her father had more grit than a beach. But this was not the same as dealing with a surly waiter or a pushy car salesman. This was dead serious, and far outside her area of expertise.

The instant she saw the open door, she ran back through the house, snagging her purse along the way, and then out the front door. Standing on the street, trembling, she whipped out her cell phone and called the first person she could think of.

Sam answered on the third ring. His voice was warm and gravelly, and she wanted to wrap it around her like a blanket. He told her very quietly, his voice as strong and hard-edged as a diamond, to go to a neighbor's house and wait for him. She didn't even consider disobeying.

Once she was at her neighbor's house—a lovely woman with two toddlers who usually chattered nonstop about babies, diapers, and things like potty training and teething—she began to realize what she'd done. She'd

29

called Sam instead of the police. Why had she done that?

Sissy brought Georgeanne a cup of hot tea, her pretty face bordering on terrified. "I've been telling Don we need to install an alarm system." She picked up her cup, her fingers trembling. In the background, her toddlers screamed along to something on the television. "What if someone tried to break in here when it's just me and the girls?"

Georgeanne willed her thumping heart to beat a little slower. "I'm sure I must have left the door unlocked," she said, wanting to calm Sissy's fears as much as her own. "Someone could have just walked right in. Or maybe I didn't push it all the way closed and it worked itself free while I was gone."

Sissy chewed her lip. "That's possible. And it's not like we've had a rash of break-ins. Still, I'll feel better once we get that alarm. Maybe we should call the police, just in case…"

Georgeanne smoothed a hand along her jeans. She'd thought about that too, but Sam just seemed like the right person. "I already called my friend. He's a badass military guy, so I know he'll make sure everything is fine. If he thinks someone broke in and I should call the police, I will."

Sissy nodded. "That sounds sensible. It's not like the police don't have enough to do, right?"

"Right."

But there was a downside to calling Sam, and Georgeanne had been thinking about that too. What if he told Rick? *Oh mercy…*

The phone chose that moment to ring and Georgeanne jumped at the blare. Sissy snatched it up and started filling her husband in. Georgeanne sat there, clutching the cup in one hand, and went over everything in her mind from the moment she'd left the house until she returned. Had she left the door unlocked? Could it have swung open from the pressure when she closed the front door?

And what did that mean for Belle? After the incident in the coffee shop, her fight-or-flight response had been so tuned that she'd ran without stopping to look for her cat. She put her head down and sucked in a breath.

She wanted to go back right now and check for Belle, but she knew better. All she could do was wait for Sam to arrive while asking herself a zillion times whether she should have just called the police instead.

Within a half hour, someone banged on the door. Georgeanne and Sissy both jumped, but then Sissy got up and went to answer it. A moment later, Sam entered the room and a wave of relief washed over Georgeanne. She didn't even hesitate before getting up and flinging herself into his arms.

He seemed stunned at first, but then his arms tightened around her. "You're fine," he said softly. "And Belle is fine too. There's no one there."

She sucked in a shaky breath and pushed herself back to look up at him. He was blurry.

"You're sure? She's really okay?"

"Yes, she's okay. She was hiding beneath the couch." His dark eyes gleamed hot, and she knew he was suppressing something. She'd always known when Sam was shoving his feelings deep and twisting the screws down on the lid.

"I want to see her. Now."

"Sure."

Georgeanne thanked Sissy, and then she and Sam went next door and into her house, which he'd locked up tight before coming over to get her. Just to be sure, he checked everything again while she cradled Belle in her arms and stroked her soft fur. Belle purred as if nothing had happened. Georgeanne was weak with relief. Belle had been her companion through all the crap with Tim, and she couldn't imagine life without her sweet cat.

Finally, Sam joined her in her office, which was in the front of the house. "You need to pack a bag, Georgie. You aren't staying here."

Her heart twisted in her chest. She wanted to do exactly as he said, and yet she'd learned a hard lesson with Tim. Never give your power to a man. Never let a man control you. She had to be strong and face her fear. Just because someone had scared her didn't mean she needed to flee. "I'm not going to run away because of a man in a coffee shop."

She'd told Sam what the man had said to her, but he hadn't yet addressed it. He stepped forward, and she realized again just how big and hard he was. In spite of herself, a little flame leapt and curled in her belly. Sam McKnight. Still so handsome. Still so remote.

And still not interested in Georgie Hayes.

Not that she needed to be worrying about that right now, but it was somehow easier to concentrate on Sam and all her latent feelings than on the fact someone had threatened her just an hour ago.

"I wasn't giving you a choice. Get packed."

Something in his tone rubbed her the wrong way, making her think of days long ago. "I'm not twelve anymore, and you can't tell me what to do. I have a life, a job." She squeezed Belle, who started to squirm. "And my cat. I can't just leave."

"Take the cat with you. But you *are* leaving, Georgie. One way or the other."

"What's that supposed to mean?"

His eyes glittered with determination. "It means I'll throw you over my shoulder if I have to."

Georgeanne swallowed. She had to be sensible about this. Had to know she was doing the right thing. "Give me a good reason, Sam. Make me believe this isn't just you being overprotective because you think you owe Rick something."

He swore then, soft and low. "All right." He put his fists on his hips, his legs spread apart. "You need to pack a bag, Georgie, and you need to come with me right now. Because I found Jake Hamilton for you—"

"You found Jake?" She'd nearly forgotten about Jake over the last couple of hours.

He nodded, his expression firm and unhappy at the same time. Dread took up residence in her gut.

"He's not coming back, Georgie."

"Something happened to him?" Her voice was little more than a whisper. She'd known it. Somehow, she'd known.

Sam nodded. "Yes."

Her eyes filled with tears and her legs just sort of collapsed underneath her. She found herself sitting on a chair, looking up at Sam through a haze of tears. "I don't understand."

He'd been a young Army sergeant working on his college degree. He'd been an intense student, a good student. She remembered him sitting in her class, always on the front row, always asking questions and taking diligent notes. He'd been the kind of person she would have said would go a long way, because he was determined to do so.

Sam came over and hunkered down in front of her. He brushed the tears off her cheeks. "I need you to trust me, Georgie. I need you to pack some things, pack the cat, and come with me."

She sucked in another breath and tried not to lose it. "I have no idea what's going on. Do you think what happened in the coffee shop was related? Was that man talking about Jake?" She had no idea why anyone would think Jake had been her lover, but right now that was the only thing that made sense. And that thought chilled her to the bone. Jake worked for a secret agency and now he was dead.

And someone had threatened her—worse, they'd actually pushed her last night.

Sam looked fierce. "I don't know, but we'll find out."

She shook her head. "I don't see how. Jake's gone, and I don't know who that guy was. Or why he thinks I know anything." She pulled in another deep breath. "I didn't do anything, Sam. I don't know what's going on and... and I'm scared."

He squeezed her hand. "I know people who can figure this out."

She knew she should ask more questions, but she was just too upset. And she trusted him. That was the bottom line. "Where are you taking me?"

"Somewhere safe."

That wasn't an answer and he knew it. And while she might have no choice in this, there was one place she didn't want to go. "I won't go to Texas, Sam. I can't—"

His fingers caressed her skin again and she found herself wanting to lean into him, wanting him to keep touching her until the sadness went away. How could her body light up when he touched her even though she was feeling so many other things right now?

"I'm not sending you to Texas. I'm not letting you out of my sight. You're coming with me, and we're going to a safe house in Maryland."

"You won't leave me?"

His smile was tender, reassuring. "No, I won't leave you."

She looked down at her lap, unable to meet the intensity of his gaze a moment longer. "All right."

His hand dropped away, and she found herself wanting to cry out, wanting to ask him not to stop.

"Good. I'm sorry about Sergeant Hamilton, Georgie. But I won't let anything happen to you. You can count on that."

"I know it." Impulsively, she reached out and ran her palm along his jaw. She'd been aching to touch him. His eyes darkened, becoming hot pools she wanted to drown in. "I trust you, Sam. Completely."

He caught her hand and pulled it away from his skin. "You can trust me with your life, Georgie. But don't make the mistake of thinking you can trust me with anything else. I'm not that good, believe me."

The car ride was silent. Or would have been if not for the incessant meowing of Georgie's cat.

"You know something, Sam?" Georgie said, and he started at the sound of her voice breaking into his thoughts when the cat had almost become white noise to him.

He shot her a glance. "What?"

"Maybe I don't want you to be good. Maybe I want you to be as bad as you can be."

Sam gripped the wheel of his truck and stared straight ahead. Jesus. "Don't say shit like that to me, Georgie. You know I'm not going there."

She snorted. "Boy, do I."

"Georgie—"

"No, don't you Georgie me. When you stopped that night..." He could feel her looking at him, her eyes boring an angry hole into him. He told himself she was reacting to everything that had happened to her today and taking it out on him. This wasn't really about something that had happened twelve years ago. It was just a convenient catalyst.

"When you stopped that night, I thought there was something wrong with me. I thought I wasn't sexy enough or special enough for you. And that hurt."

"Of course you were," he bit out. "But you're Rick's little sister and I was the wrong guy for a lot of reasons. I stopped because you *were* special."

"You were the one I wanted."

He swallowed hard. "I couldn't do it, Georgie. I couldn't do it and look Rick in the eye ever again. Or your parents."

She didn't say anything for a long moment. "You know who was my first?"

"Goddamn it, I don't want to know." His voice

snapped in the interior of the car. Even the cat went silent. Sam closed his eyes. He did not lose his temper. Not ever. But she made him forget all the vows he'd ever sworn to himself.

Georgie folded her arms over her chest. "Fine. But you know what you need to remember right now? Here it is, so put it front and center in that brain of yours and keep it there. I'm not *your* sister, and I'm not a kid anymore."

Sam sat there in stony silence, uncertain what in the hell he could possibly say. No, she wasn't his sister. But it was safer for him if he thought of her that way. He wanted to keep her in a safe place in his head, but in the space of a conversation she'd gone and thrown her grappling hook over the walls he'd erected and torn them right down.

She thought he had trouble remembering she wasn't a kid anymore. No, what he had trouble remembering was that he was no good for her. Because damn if he didn't want her. He wanted her every possible way he could have her.

But she wasn't his for the taking. She was too good for the likes of him. Even if he wanted something more than a few nights of sex with her—and he in no way thought he did—he owed the Hayeses too much to drag their daughter into the kind of life he led. Now that he'd joined HOT, his already crazy life had just gotten crazier. His deployments would be more specialized now, more dangerous in many ways. With the Rangers, he'd done plenty of dangerous things—jumping into enemy territory in the middle of the night and engaging in pitched battles with enemy forces while trying to take—or defend—ground.

But HOT, like Delta Force, was about a hundred levels up. Their missions were top secret, highly focused, and extremely sensitive. Right now, most of their resources were bent toward catching Jassar ibn-Rashad. The new Freedom Force leader had escaped a mission to capture him just a few months ago now. Two men were killed in that op—Marco San Ramos and Jim Matuzaki. Sam was one of the replacements, and he felt it keenly. The other guys didn't talk much about what had happened in the desert, but everyone knew. The entire squad was captured, and Jim and Marco were executed when no one would talk.

The rest of them would have been executed too, except that another HOT squad managed to get them out. Sam hadn't gone out on an op with them yet, but it could happen at any moment.

Now, however, he had Georgie to worry about. When the Kid had found out that Jake Hamilton had been dragged out of the Potomac only a few days ago, Sam's blood ran cold. Right after that, Georgie called him, terrified, and Sam bolted out of HOT HQ like someone had aimed a flamethrower at his ass.

Sam's phone rang and he glanced down at it sitting in the console. A HOT code flashed on the screen so he picked it up and answered with a clipped, "McKnight."

"This is Captain Girard, Sergeant. Everything okay?"

Sam's gut hollowed. His CO calling him couldn't be a good thing at a time like this. "Yessir. Just have to take care of something personal, sir."

"Big Mac told me about your friend. She okay?"

Sam glanced over at Georgie, who was now staring out the window. Mad at him, no doubt. "I think so, sir. There was no one in the house, but the back door had been forced."

Georgie swung around to look at him, her eyes wide. Yeah, he hadn't told her that part. And she was gonna give him hell over it.

"Circumstances have changed somewhat, Sergeant. It seems as if HOT is officially involved in this case now. You'll need to bring her here, and then we'll make sure she gets somewhere safe."

Sam gripped the phone tight. Jesus, if HOT was involved, there was most certainly a foreign component. The military did not operate inside US borders except under very specific and well-defined circumstances. This was not one of them. And that made Sam's blood run just a little colder. What the hell had Georgie gotten herself into?

"I need to do this, sir. I'm responsible for her." Because Rick would kill him if anything happened to Georgie. Hell, Sam would hand him the gun and beg him to pull the trigger.

There was a moment of silence on the other end of the phone. "Fine. But you're coming here first. Understood, soldier?"

"Sir, yessir," Sam replied. The connection ended and Sam put the phone down again with a sinking feeling in his gut. If HOT was a part of this thing, the level of severity had just taken a quantum leap.

He glanced over at Georgie. She had her lower lip between her teeth. "You didn't tell me about the door."

"Didn't want to worry you."

She frowned. "I was already worried, Sam."

"I know. That's why I didn't want to add to it."

She let out an exasperated breath. "Always trying to protect me, even when I don't want it."

He flexed his hands on the wheel. "You want it this time, Georgie. Believe me."

"I don't suppose you're going to tell me what that means?"

He shook his head slowly. "Nope. And don't ask again, because I can't. It's not my decision."

"Does this have anything to do with Jake's death?"

"I think it has everything to do with it," he said softly.

Georgie turned her head and stared out the window. She didn't speak again.

FOUR

GEORGEANNE STOOD ON THE SCREENED-IN back porch of a small cottage on the Eastern Shore of Maryland, arms folded over her chest, staring out at the creek running past the house. It was late afternoon and the sun gleamed golden on the water. A blue heron picked its way along the shore on the opposite side, and marsh grass waved occasionally in the slight breeze called up whenever a bird took flight.

This was not at all what she'd expected to be doing when she'd awakened this morning. But now she was here, and her head was still reeling from everything she'd been through. She heard a sound behind her and turned as Sam strolled outside. He'd changed out of his military uniform and into a pair of faded jeans that sat low on his hips. He wore a navy T-shirt that clung to the broad muscles of his tattooed biceps and chest and made her mouth water.

Tattoos? Sam hadn't had tattoos before. A black tribal design appeared to surround his right bicep. She couldn't tell what was on his left, but she saw a hint of ink when he crossed his arms over his chest.

lump in her throat. "I don't understand why Jake's dead. Or what it has to do with me."

Sam ran a hand through his hair and let out a breath. "Jake was involved in things he shouldn't have been involved in. And it looks like he had a crush on you, G. He had pictures of you in his apartment, poems he'd written. Whoever killed him thinks you know something about what he was doing."

Georgeanne wanted to howl. Instead, she shuddered. It was creepy to think Jake had had a crush on her and now he was dead. "But I *don't* know anything. I didn't even know Jake that well. He took three classes from me, that's it. We had coffee a few times, but it was during my office hours. It wasn't a date or anything."

"He seemed to think it was. Others did too, if what this guy said to you was any indication."

She shook her head, wanting to deny everything Sam was saying. "But Jake was a good guy. Harmless. I can't believe he was mixed up in something bad."

"You aren't that naïve, Georgie. Just because someone is nice doesn't mean they haven't done something wrong. I'm sorry when anyone dies so senselessly, but trust me when I tell you he wasn't minding his own business when it happened."

Georgeanne swallowed the lump in her throat. "So now you get to say when someone deserves the bad things that happen to them? I think that's rather cynical, don't you?"

Sam's expression was stark. "I've seen too much in this life not to be cynical. Jake Hamilton was doing things he shouldn't have been doing. And while I'm sorry you're hurt over this, I'm more pissed that he managed to drag you into it. You're lucky they didn't succeed with the train last night."

She closed her eyes, feeling the ache in her hip anew. "I know. And I'm sorry. But I liked Jake. Or at least the Jake I knew. It's not easy to start believing he was a bad person."

"I didn't say he was bad. But he did bad things. Or stupid things, at least. And that cost him his life."

She looked up at him. "And I'm mixed up in it."

Sam nodded. "We don't know precisely how. It could just be that they think you were his girlfriend and know something about what he was doing. He might have said something to them, might have implicated you in some way. Did he ever give you anything?"

She shook her head. "Tests and papers. Nothing else." She chewed on her bottom lip. "The last time I saw him, he was with a man in the Metro. It was late, and I was waiting for the train home. Jake said he was going to Crystal City with a friend. Then a man showed up and they started talking."

Sam's gaze had sharpened. "And what was unusual in that?"

She blinked. "I don't know that anything was."

"You mentioned it. I think you wouldn't have done that if it didn't bother you somehow."

Her heart beat a little faster as she thought back to that night. "The man seemed angry. And I didn't like the way he looked at me." She shrugged. "It was nothing else, really. Just a bad feeling he gave me."

"Did you talk to him?"

"No."

"What did he look like?"

"Dark. Middle-Eastern, maybe, and that pains me to say because it shouldn't mean a damn thing."

"No, it shouldn't. But sometimes it does." He didn't have to remind her that she'd described the man from the coffee shop as vaguely foreign, too.

"He had a goatee, closely cropped. He looked… very manicured. Well-dressed and well-groomed. There was nothing unusual in that, except that he didn't seem to match Jake, if you know what I mean. Jake was, I don't know, very casual. Except when in uniform, of course."

"You have something or saw something. Or someone thinks so anyway. And until we figure out what that is, you're staying here."

A little wave of panic rose in her chest. "You aren't leaving me out here alone, are you?" She'd lived alone for the past year, but being left in a remote location in Maryland where she didn't know a soul and couldn't even see the next house? The thought terrified her.

Sam put his hands on her shoulders. "I'm not leaving you. I'm here until this is over. And if I have to leave for some reason, one of the other guys will be with you. We won't leave you unprotected."

Georgeanne shivered. His hands on her shoulders were warm and strong, and she wanted to feel them everywhere, wanted the heat of him to engulf her. She hated that she did, especially when he seemed so determined to be remote. "Who are those guys?"

"My coworkers," he said, his tone telling her he wouldn't say anything else. "They know what they're doing."

She grinned up at him suddenly. "Careful, Sam, or I'll start to think you're part of some secret military outfit."

He gazed at her steadily, his expression never changing, and it suddenly hit her that that was exactly what was going on. Sam McKnight was a part of something she wasn't supposed to know about.

"Does Rick know?" she asked, and his gaze shuttered.

He turned away from her, his jaw tight. She didn't know why she felt closer to him in that moment, but she did. He was a part of something big and she was the only one who'd guessed, even if he wouldn't admit it.

She touched his arm. "I won't say a word. I promise."

"There's nothing to say, Georgie. I'm a Ranger. Same as always."

"Of course," she said. But she didn't believe it.

Sam was restless as hell. Evening was falling and frogs began their nightly chorus against the backdrop of the river and marshes nearby. There was no car noise out here, no planes or motorcycles or people talking. It was peaceful, but he didn't feel at peace.

Georgie sat at the small table on the porch with her laptop. They hadn't spoken much in a couple of hours now. He hadn't known what to say to her, truth be told. Georgie wasn't stupid and of course she would figure there was something going on after he'd taken her to HOT HQ. It wasn't that they didn't bring civilians to HOT—they did, clearly, or there wouldn't be a separate area for visitors—but he hadn't expected to have to take her there.

The cover story was always that they were Rangers when in truth they were so much more. HOT was secret, its members recruited from the Rangers, the Green Berets—and even from Delta Force, which was very similar. The wives of HOT members didn't even know about its existence, though they knew their husbands went on missions quite often. HOT was, by design, a male-dominated organization. That's just how Special Operations were, though with women being allowed to do combat tours nowadays, he didn't think it would be long before they had female team members too.

Sam had gone out into the front yard to place a call back to HOT. He'd told them what Georgie had said about the guy with Jake Hamilton. It was probably nothing, but Sam had learned not to discount anything out of hand. Explore every lead, no matter how insignificant.

What he hadn't told Georgie—what he couldn't tell her—was that Jake Hamilton had been attempting to sell information about a DARPA mini-UAV project to a foreign organization. Mini-drones were the size of moths or hummingbirds, and they could do amazing surveillance work. They could also be weaponized, which was a frightening fucking thought. But the problem with them was powering them for long periods of time. They just didn't have long-range capability. Their juice drained within minutes.

And that's what DARPA was working on. A mini-drone, capable of being weaponized and able to fly long distances before recharging. That was the nightmare: a weapon of that scope in the wrong hands could change the face of the War on Terror—and not in a good way.

Mendez had said during the briefing that they still

didn't know if Jake had managed the hand-off or not, but the group he'd been dealing with was apparently a front for the Freedom Force. They didn't think Hamilton had known precisely who he was selling the information to. Or cared.

He may not have been a particularly stylish dude, according to Georgie, but he sure had expensive tastes in things other than clothes. A vintage Corvette, for instance. A rare Colt pistol. Front row seats to a Gina Domerico concert.

Fucking dumbass.

The Freedom Force probably wasn't interested in the time and money required to build a mini-drone—but they would be interested in selling the information to the highest bidder. Most likely, they'd attempt to exchange it for a small tactical nuke. If he were Ibn-Rashad, that's what he'd do. Get a nuke and detonate it somewhere in Europe, preferably near a US base.

Matt Girard told Sam to hold tight and they'd get back to him when they had something. Which left Sam with a whole lot of nothing to do, except sit around in a remote cottage with the one woman in this world he shouldn't touch.

Georgie looked up from her computer, as if she'd known he was thinking about her. Their gazes clashed and held, and his heart ticked up a few beats. He didn't know what to say to her anymore. Hell, he hadn't known what to say to her since the minute she'd walked into that bowling alley in Hopeful and tied his tongue into knots.

He'd been filled with conflicting feelings, and he was still filled with them. She was just about the sexiest woman he'd ever known, and he knew that a lot of that was the

that."

"I'll try."

"Good."

He blew out a breath. "I wasn't right for you then. I hope you realize that. I wasn't in a good place, and I didn't want to hurt you."

"You might not have wanted to, but you did anyway. Self-esteem can be a fragile thing at that age, and you shattered mine pretty badly when you pushed me away."

"I was trying to do the right thing."

"I know that now." She took a bite of the pasta to cover her raw nerves. "Oh my God, this is good. So much better than sex."

It wasn't a good segue, but it would have to do. Because it didn't do any good to talk about the past with Sam. She still felt like the annoying little kid. And the fact that he'd been trying to protect her when he'd turned her away twelve years ago? It only made her heart squeeze a little tighter and her emotions twist into knots.

Sam shook his head and laughed. "Now you're just trying to bait me into saying something contradictory."

"Maybe." She took another bite and closed her eyes. "Or maybe not. Seriously, who needs a man when you have this? It's an orgasm on a plate."

"You're laying it on a little thick, G."

She grinned at him. "So you think. But really, sex is a bit overrated. Even you have to admit that. We get all worked up based on our hormones—and then what? It feels nice for a while and then it's over." She shrugged. "I've been living without it for over a year now, and I'm no worse off."

Intense dark eyes raked over her face and something

throbbed deep inside her. Suddenly, sex seemed a whole lot more important than she wanted it to be.

"Eat the pasta, G, and shut the hell up."

"You're growling again," she said.

He only glared at her.

There was a thunderstorm later that night. The crack of thunder and sizzle of ozone woke Georgeanne up. She bolted up in bed, feeling disoriented until she remembered where she was. Sam was on a fold-up Army cot in the living room. He'd given her the bed and stationed himself in the small room right off the front door. She didn't ask if he was armed. She didn't have to.

He must have seen the concern on her face because he'd told her it was simply SOP—standard operating procedure. He didn't expect a threat, but he prepared for one because that's what he did.

She'd gone to bed feeling only marginally better since she suspected he wouldn't tell her the truth anyway. There could be a whole boatload of bad guys out there and he wouldn't let her know it. Except she had to admit that she was pretty confident in the men she'd met earlier today. They were on top of this, whatever this was, and they'd find the person who killed Jake.

Thunder cracked again, and Belle scrambled under the bed. Georgeanne threw the covers back and went into the bathroom. When she came out, she realized she'd drunk the bottle of water she'd set on her bedside table, so she went into the kitchen to get another one.

She could see Sam lying on the cot, one arm thrown over his face, the other beside him. Lightning flashed and illuminated the dark room for a split second, and Georgeanne had to stifle the groan on her lips.

God, he was beautiful. He lay on top of the covers, clad in a pair of shorts, and his bare chest was a sight to behold. Far more muscular than when he'd been seventeen—or even twenty-one. And he was inked. She couldn't tell what the designs were in that brief flash of light, but she'd seen them there and they made her mouth go dry.

What would it be like to trace them with her tongue? Wetness flooded her at the thought, and her temperature kicked up a degree. She'd told him sex was overrated— and she hadn't been kidding, but what if it wasn't overrated with him? What if he possessed the ability to make her feel something more than just the sweetness of a release?

Georgeanne shivered with awareness. It had been so long since a man had touched her. So long since she'd cared. And now here she was, panting over the one man who had always seemed determined not to have anything to do with her.

Compelled by a force she didn't understand, she crept toward the cot. She just wanted to see him up close, wanted to know if the ripple of muscle was as impressive as it had seemed in that flash of light. Wanted to see him breathing and know he was really here and that she wasn't somehow imagining the whole thing in a fevered dream.

"What are you doing?"

His voice startled her. She stopped, clutching her water bottle, and swallowed. "Just making sure you're okay."

He removed his arm from over his face. She could see the glitter of his eyes in the darkness. "I'm fine."

He sounded prickly, as usual, and it got to her. "Your virtue is safe with me, Sam. You don't have to get all edgy about it. I wasn't coming over to take advantage of you or anything."

He swung his legs to the floor and sat up. "I'm not worried about my virtue."

"No, you're worried about mine. Or about what Rick or my parents would think if you did what you really want to do."

He tilted his head to the side. "How do you know what I really want to do? Maybe I'm not attracted to you. Did you ever consider that?"

She felt those words like a blow. After everything with Tim, after the heartbreak and betrayal, the idea that yet another man found her less than appealing hurt more than she could say. Yes, she'd done it to herself. She'd poked and prodded and pushed, and for what? So he could tell her he didn't want her? So she could suffer the sting of humiliation yet one more time?

Georgeanne couldn't think of one damn thing to say. Instead, she turned on her heel and fled back toward the bedroom. She was inside, throwing the door closed, when a big shape wedged itself between the door and the jamb. She didn't fight; she just let go and stepped back, arms around herself as he loomed big in the room.

Thunder crashed harder than before, but she didn't take her attention from Sam.

"Goddamn you, Georgie," he said softly. "You push and push and push, and then when I push back, when I try like hell to keep you from making a mistake, I say something so fucking rotten even I can't believe I said it." He shook his head. "I'm sorry, I didn't mean it. You're beautiful and hot, and any man would be crazy not to want you."

She held up a hand. "Stop. I don't want to hear another word. You don't mean it." She sucked in a tear-soaked breath and swore she wasn't breaking down and making her humiliation complete. "I know you're just trying to make me feel better. And it's my fault for putting you in that position. I do keep pushing, and I don't know why. Maybe it's Tim and the marriage…" Here she actually had to swallow down a load of tears. "…and the humiliation of being left for someone else. I don't know, but you have my word I won't do it again."

His voice, when he spoke, was low and hoarse, as if it were being dragged from him. "I do want you, Georgie. I've wanted you since that night twelve years ago. I want to spread you out beneath me and make you come so many times you can't do it anymore. I want to taste your pussy and feel your legs wrapped around me as I pound into you. I want to see you swallow my cock and hear you cry out in ecstasy. I want all those things, and the only reason I don't take them is because you deserve better. I can't give you anything, Georgie. I'm nothing, nobody—"

She closed the distance between them and put her hand over his mouth. "Shut up, Sam. Shut the fuck up right now. You *are* somebody. To *me*. You always have been, dammit. I've loved you since I was thirteen, and I'm not an idiot. Rick loves you. My parents love you. None of us are stupid." She was crying now, the tears flowing freely down her cheeks. She put her hands on either side of his face, cupped his hard jaw with shaking fingers. "You aren't a nobody, Sam. You're amazing and wonderful and perfect just the way you are. And if your parents couldn't see that, if they made you think differently, then you need to believe me and not them. Because I'm right, dammit, and they're the ones who're stupid."

He spanned the back of her head with one broad hand. She could feel the tremors running through his body as he held her there. "You're so fucking sweet, Georgeanne. I've always wanted you, since I first noticed you grew breasts. I've had a helluva time keeping my hands off you all these years. But I had to do it. You were meant for more than I could give you, and I couldn't disrespect your parents that way. They trusted me. I couldn't break that trust."

Her breasts were tingling, her nipples tightening, and her core had grown impossibly wet. "They aren't here now," she said, stepping into his big body, bringing her aching breasts in contact with his naked chest. The thin cotton of her pajama top wasn't much of a barrier, but it felt like the most torturous wall between them at the moment. "And even if they were in the next room, they have no say in my life. Nor should they have a say in yours. We're adults, Sam. We do what we want. With whom we want."

"I know that, but—"

She put her hand over his mouth to stop him from talking, from ruining this moment. She needed this. Needed him. So damn much. She'd felt empty for so long, and here was this man who made her feel like a sexual being again.

"No one is here but you and me, and no one ever has to know if that's what you really want. What I want is you—inside me, making me come. Making me feel like

I'm beautiful again. Like I'm worth wanting."

She didn't think he would do anything, but then he lowered his head slowly, almost as if he were fighting with himself. Right before he kissed her, he muttered against her mouth, "Tim was a fucking idiot, do you hear me? No woman is more beautiful than you."

SIX

HE WAS DAMNED. HE KNEW it, and he didn't really care right this moment. Georgeanne Hayes was in his arms, her pretty body pressed tight up against his, and he didn't fucking care about anything but that.

Her mouth parted beneath his and his tongue slipped inside, drew her into a delicious stroking that made his body harden even more than it already was. She said he was worthwhile, important, and he believed her. For right now anyway, he believed her.

He'd fought himself twelve years ago, and he'd fought himself today—Jesus, was it just today?—and he wasn't fighting anymore. Georgie knew what she wanted and he was going to give it to her, at least once before he died. He couldn't have her in his life permanently, because his life was too unpredictable, but he could have this.

Georgie's hands roamed over his hot flesh and then slid beneath his shorts until she grasped him. He groaned softly, his body so hard it hurt. Her hand was small and soft as she stroked him and pleasure began to sing inside his brain. He felt the familiar tightening at the base of his spine and knew he had to stop her before he embarrassed himself and came before he ever got inside her.

He broke the kiss and pushed her back until he could pull off her little pajama top and matching shorts. Her curves beckoned, a banquet for his hands and eyes and mouth.

"Oh, Georgeanne, the things I want to do to you," he said, his voice a soft sizzle in the night.

"Don't talk about it, Sam. Just do it."

"Remember you asked for it," he said, pushing her back onto the bed and coming down on top of her. He nipped her earlobe, slid his tongue along the column of her throat, and then fastened his mouth around one tight nipple while she gasped and arched herself into him.

Her fingers clutched his shoulders, dug into his muscles, and he loved the feel of it. Loved that she clung to him, making little noises while he sucked her nipple. He alternated the pressure, a little soft, a little hard, finding just the right amount she liked. Then he moved to her other nipple and repeated the performance.

He slid a hand down her smooth skin, came to the mound of her sex—and found it clean-shaven. He nearly choked on his own tongue at that little discovery. He could feel her panting and, yes, even laughing a little.

"Not what you expected?"

He left her breasts and trailed his mouth down her abdomen. "No. It's very naughty of you, Georgeanne. Very sexy."

"I'd tell you I did it for you, but that would be a lie. I did it for me. Because I wanted to, because I like the way it looks and feels. It's the only thing that's made me feel sexy these past few months."

He reached her mound and placed a kiss there. "You are sexy. Incredibly sexy." He ran a finger down the seam of her pussy. "So hot and wet, Georgeanne. What do you want me to do about it?"

"I want you inside me."

"All in good time." He pushed her legs open and settled between them. And then he ran his tongue the length of her pussy while she cried out.

She tasted like honey to him—sweet, sweet honey. He spread her open with his fingers and licked his way around her slick folds. And then he touched the point of his tongue to her clit and she arched up off the bed with a sharp cry. He held his tongue against her while she writhed, stunned that she'd come so quickly.

When her tremors subsided, he built the tension again, this time adding his fingers to the mix, sliding in and out of her with short, hard strokes. She shattered again, his name a broken sound on her lips.

It was the most beautiful sound he'd ever heard, and he'd heard a lot of women say his name in bed. But none of them were Georgie.

He kissed his way up her body, his hands gliding over her sweet soft skin, learning her by touch, mapping her for his memory so that he could call up these moments later, when she was out of his life again. So he could remember how it felt to make love to Georgeanne Hayes.

"You'd better not be planning to leave now that you've made me come."

Her skin was slick with perspiration, and he laughed low in his throat. "Oh no, not this time. I'm too hungry for you."

"Thank God for small favors."

He levered up and yanked off his shorts and underwear, and then he reached into the bedside stand and knew he'd find condoms. Leave it to HOT to think of everything. He tore one open and rolled it on. He could hear Georgie breathing rapidly, and he leaned down to kiss her.

"I don't want to hurt you," he said.

"I doubt you're *that* big."

He couldn't believe that she could make him laugh at a time like this. "I'm thinking of your hip, smartass."

"I'll let you know, but right now I think it hurts worse not to have you where I want you."

He sucked a nipple into his mouth again, held himself over her, his cock just nudging her slick folds. He wanted to plunge home and keep plunging until he was nothing but a mass of raw nerve endings, but more than that, he didn't want to hurt her already bruised body.

"Sam, please. I've been waiting twelve years. Longer, if you consider when I first knew what sex was about."

"All the more reason to take our time." He slid just inside her, held steady while she writhed beneath him. "You're hot, Georgie. So fucking hot. It's everything I can do to do this right."

"There is no right way or wrong way. There's only you and me and this amazing feeling that I'll die if you don't make me come again."

He slid just a little deeper. "I thought you said sex was overrated."

"It still might be. But I won't know until you actually do something to me."

Sam shook his head even as his balls began to ache with the need to plunge into her. "I thought I did something. Didn't you just come?"

"Yeah, and I'm greedy for more." She sucked in a breath and he could hear the tears in her voice. "I've felt undesirable to anyone for so long I almost forgot how good it could feel to have a man in my bed."

He leaned down and kissed her. "Shh, Georgie, it's all right. I'm not leaving until you're completely satisfied."

She lifted her hips and tried to get him to go deeper. He gave her a little more length. She curled a leg around his hip.

"Is this the injured one?" he asked, hooking his arm behind her knee.

"No."

"Good." He pushed her leg up until it was brushing his shoulder, opening her wide. And then he sank the rest of the way inside her.

"Oh my God, that's good," she gasped.

He held himself still, afraid he'd lose it if he didn't. "Yeah." He couldn't manage another word. He was deep inside Georgeanne Hayes, the perfect little princess of his teenage years, and he wanted to corrupt her utterly. He wanted to possess her and make her scream his name. He wanted to imprint himself on her so thoroughly she'd never forget this night with him.

He turned his head and pressed a kiss to her calf. He could feel her inner muscles gripping him, urging him forward, but he held still and just enjoyed the feeling of being inside her at last.

Lightning flashed outside the window, and her face was illuminated for a long second. Her head was thrown back, her eyes closed, her lower lip between her teeth. She looked utterly beautiful and completely lost in the moment.

"Look at me," he commanded, because he couldn't stand for her to be lost in her own world without him. He needed that touchstone, needed to see her eyes and know she was with *him*, with Sam McKnight, and not just the first man to touch her since Tim Cash had broken her heart.

Her eyes snapped open and the lightning flashed again. He saw exactly what he was looking for—raw need, all for him. He began to move, pulling out of her slowly, slamming back in just a little harder each time.

"Oh," she said, again and again. "Oh *yessss*."

Sam rocked into her faster, harder, deeper. Intensely. He let go of her leg, changed the angle at which he entered her, and listened to her beg him for yet more. He was mindless, a machine, a creature who existed solely to pleasure this one woman. He wanted her sighs and moans, her breathy gasps, her screams. He wanted everything she had to give, and he would do anything to get it.

His body was on fire with sensation. All his pleasure centered on his balls, his cock, on the slick pressure of Georgie's body surrounding him. He couldn't remember the last time it had been this good, though it must have been. He loved sex, loved pleasuring a woman, and loved the ultimate payoff when he finally let himself go.

But he couldn't for the life of him recall it feeling quite this good before.

Georgie arched up off the bed and tugged his head down for a kiss, a hot, wet melding of tongues that was not unlike the melding of their bodies. He sucked her tongue into his mouth, nipping her lower lip.

"Sam—oh God, Sam. Please, please… I need…"

He knew what she needed. What he needed.

He withdrew from her body, urged her up and onto her knees. She bent over and gripped her pillow, her ass in the air, and Sam couldn't help but take a moment to run his fingers over her naked folds. So pretty, so hot. Georgie whimpered then and he positioned himself, plunging deep inside her. The angle was different here, but still so good. He loved the sight of his body disappearing into hers, the sounds their bodies made as he rocked into her.

He ran a finger over her clit and felt her shiver. He skimmed it again and again, enjoyed the way she worked her body against his fingers, seeking more pleasure. Her inner muscles tightened, clamping him almost painfully as the pressure built inside her. He could feel her release beginning and he pumped into her harder. At the last second, his thumb skimmed the tight bud of her anus, pressing ever so lightly on that most sensitive of spots.

She flew apart with a long cry, his name a sob as her body shuddered and bucked against him. He pushed her forward against the mattress even more, pushing her thighs together until his were on the outside of hers. She gripped him so tightly as he drove into her again and again, until the pressure in his balls just frigging exploded. He came hard, his body flying apart, dissolving.

When he came back to himself, he was on top of Georgie, who was sprawled against the mattress now, his cock still deep inside her, still twitching as her inner walls spasmed against him from time to time. They were both panting and sweating and the storm was still raging outside, though farther away now.

He pushed himself up and off her. He wanted nothing more than to collapse and sleep for the next fourteen hours or so, but he had to remove the condom. He got up and went into the bathroom and then when he came back, he hesitated. She was still on her belly, still sprawled across the mattress, and he suddenly felt like an ass for using her so roughly.

He'd fucked her dirty, as if she'd wanted it that way when he knew nothing of the sort, and he wished he could start over, do it right this time. She was too precious, too special to treat so casually.

She turned her head, saw him standing there, and rolled onto her side. Her body glistened in the moonlight that streamed into the room now that the storm had passed over. She was curvy, perfectly made, and he wanted to fall to his knees and worship her, beg her forgiveness for daring to use her for his pleasure.

"That," she said softly, "was fucking *amazing*."

Georgeanne's body ached, but in a good way. Oh, her hip was pretty sore, but she wouldn't trade a moment of what had just happened for less pain. She frowned as she realized Sam was staring at her in that way of his that never meant well for her in the end. He was brooding about something when all she wanted was to wrap herself around him and go to sleep for a few hours so she could wake up and do it all over again.

"I was too rough," he said brusquely. "I should have taken better care of you."

Georgeanne pushed herself up to a sitting position.

"What, are you kidding me? Did you just hear a word I said?"

He was standing there, not moving, and she took the opportunity to let her gaze slide over his naked body. Oh. My. God.

He was beautiful, big and muscled, with tattoos on his chest and biceps. His abs were tight and defined, his hipbones made her want to bite them, and his cock was still half-hard.

And completely beautiful. She didn't have tons of experience with men—oh, she'd been to college and she'd been married to Tim, but no lover she could remember had been quite as satisfying. Sam knew how to use his body to get the most out of hers; that was for sure.

"You don't have to pretend, Georgie. I was rough with you."

"If that was rough, I want it again just as soon as possible."

He came over and stood beside the bed, his eyes on hers. "You aren't just saying that?"

She got up on her knees and put her palms against his chest. "Sam, my God, no." She slid her hands over him, felt the smooth ridges of muscle, the nicks and dings of scar tissue where he'd been injured. She was so damned emotional right now, and it was all because of him. Because she'd felt like there was something wrong with her, like she wasn't all that desirable. Tim had left her for another woman. How could she not take that personally? How could she not think there was something wrong with *her* response in bed? If she couldn't satisfy Tim, who had fairly vanilla tastes, what did that say about her?

But then Sam had just made love to her in ways that

were a revelation. He hadn't treated her like a princess on a pedestal. He'd treated her like a woman with earthy tastes and needs, and she'd loved every moment of it. He hadn't been rough, or even particularly kinky—he'd just been wrapped up in the moment, and so had she.

And she damn well wanted more of the same.

"Don't lie, Georgie. Because if you don't tell me the truth, I'll do it again. I'll start out wanting to be gentle, wanting to take you carefully, and I'll end up forgetting and just taking you however I feel like."

She shivered. "Oh wow, I sure hope so."

He closed his eyes and tilted his head back and she pressed her mouth to his pec. She hadn't gotten to taste him earlier, and she'd desperately wanted to. His skin was hot, salty, and she ran her tongue down to his nipple, swirling around it.

His breath hissed in. "You're making me hard."

Her stomach hollowed with need. "Oh goodie. Because I want you again, Sam. I need you to make me come." She kissed his chest. "Over." She moved her mouth lower. "And over." She moved lower still. "And over…"

SEVEN

WHEN GEORGEANNE WOKE AGAIN, THE sun was up and Sam was gone. She could hear him banging around in the kitchen, so she wasn't worried. She stretched, her body rippling with pleasure.

Sam was a force to be reckoned with in bed. And she was surprised to learn that she wasn't far behind. She wanted to experience everything with him. She wanted his passion, his incredible body, his intense focus. When Sam made love to her, he committed himself fully to the act.

His tongue and teeth were magic—as were his fingers, his cock, and the way he just knew how to touch her or move inside her at precisely the right moment. He'd made her scream his name too many times to count. He'd talked dirty to her when she'd tentatively asked him to. She hadn't been sure if he would—or even if she would like it—but my God, the way her body clenched when he whispered that he was going to fuck her hard and fast. She'd shattered with little more incentive than those words and his body deep inside hers.

She was, she was discovering, adventurous and enthusiastic. It was such a revelation after the last several years that she wanted to call Tim and Lindsey and tell them to kiss her ass.

She wouldn't, of course, because ladies did not act that way. She stifled a giggle when she thought of her beauty queen mother instructing her on proper etiquette and the ways in which a true lady behaved.

A true lady probably didn't ride her lover's cock with abandon or beg him to suck her nipples hard while she came either. Both of those were things that Georgeanne had done last night.

And she wasn't sorry for it, either.

She got up and went into the bathroom, brushed her teeth, and took a very quick shower before slipping into a maxi dress and piling her hair on top of her head. When she went into the kitchen in search of coffee, Sam was there, his back to her, scrambling eggs and fixing toast, and her heart just sort of melted.

He was shirtless and he had a tribal tattoo that spread from his shoulder to the small of his back. She hadn't noticed last night because she hadn't exactly been looking there.

"Wow, that must have hurt," she said.

He glanced at her, and her heart sort of skipped a little bit. He didn't look like he was cutting himself away from her, but he didn't look as open as he had in bed either. She knew what he was thinking about. Or she thought she knew.

In the broad light of day, he'd be thinking pretty hard about her family and how it was some kind of a betrayal to sleep with her. Which was ridiculous considering they were adults and this wasn't the Middle Ages, but it was still so much like Sam to be concerned about her family. She wanted to kiss him senseless and smack him silly at the same time.

And then she wanted to wrap herself around him and never let go.

That thought gave her pause, because it was a pretty intense thought. Yeah, she'd been in love with him once, but she'd done a whole lot of living since then. She wasn't the same naïve girl she used to be, and love wasn't something she could ever approach with the same innocence she once had. She'd been burned by it too badly.

Besides, you couldn't be in love with a man you'd barely spoken to in twelve years, even if he had given you pretty much the best sex of your life. She loved him as a friend. Always had, always would. But more? Not likely.

"Things worth having often hurt. And yeah, tattoos fucking hurt."

"So why do it?"

He shrugged. "Because I wanted to."

"Sounds like a good enough reason to me."

He turned around and set a plate with eggs and toast on the counter in front of her. "You all about doing things because you want to do them now?"

He was mocking her, so she stuck her tongue out at him. She didn't miss the way his eyes darkened or the way her pulse kicked up in response. "I'm a free spirit, Sam. I go where the wind blows me."

"Where's it blowing you today?"

She arched an eyebrow. "I think it'll blow me to my laptop to grade papers. Then it'll blow me outside for a look at the water, maybe a short walk. Then it'll probably blow my clothes right off."

"You planning to be inside or outside when that happens?"

She shrugged. "Depends, I guess."

"On what?"

"On where you are in relation to me and how badly I need your cock inside me."

He closed his eyes then and swallowed. "Georgie, when you say things like that…"

"Makes you hard, right?"

"Makes me fucking crazy. Makes me want things…"

"What kind of things?"

He turned away from her and poured some coffee. "Eat your eggs, Georgie."

She forked some into her mouth and swallowed. "You're a mess, Sam McKnight. But you sure are a hot mess."

She was driving him crazy. Sam didn't remember ever being so wound up over a woman in his life, though he knew that a large part of it was the fact this was Georgeanne Hayes and he'd decided a long time ago that she was off-limits to him. He was having a hard time remembering why he'd decided such a thing when he thought about the two of them in bed together, but then he remembered they were here in this cottage because she was in trouble and he was supposed to be protecting her. That made him remember why his kind of life wasn't right for a woman like her.

She was a college professor and a friend, and she was still hurting from her divorce. How could he possibly be what she needed in her life right now? He shouldn't have touched her last night—but he'd been unable to stop himself. She'd been so wounded and vulnerable, and he'd just wanted her to know that she was perfect in his eyes.

Tim Cash was a douchebag. How could he screw around on a woman like Georgie? He'd had everything and he'd fucked it up. Sam couldn't imagine how Tim could have wanted another woman when he'd had Georgie in his bed.

Jesus. A part of Sam wanted to rewind the clock and take back everything that had happened last night, so he wouldn't feel this damn guilt wrapping around his soul when he thought of explaining what he'd done to Rick.

"I'm worried about her, Sam. Can you check on her?"

"Sure thing, bro. While I'm at it, I'll fuck her for good measure."

Sam gritted his teeth. Yeah, like that's what he'd say to her brother. But it's how he felt. Like he'd betrayed their friendship in some way when he'd used Georgie for his own gratification.

Yet he still wanted to strip her down to her bare skin and lay her out on the nearest flat surface so he could touch and taste and feel his way to bliss one more time. She'd rocked his world last night, and not just because she said things that shocked him—because she was Georgie and she was supposed to be prim and proper—but also because she was so honest and real with her feelings. She believed in him, and that both terrified him and buoyed him at the same time.

Not many people in his life had ever believed in him. The Hayeses had, but he had to imagine they wouldn't be pleased about him and Georgie. Not that there was a him and Georgie. Still, he knew what kind of life she was supposed to have, what kind of life they wanted her to come back to Texas for, and he had absolutely no place in it.

Georgie was meant to be lording it over the Junior League while tending her three perfect children, maintaining her McMansion in the right part of town, and making love to her happy husband every night.

Jesus, and wasn't that just perfectly sexist of him? He tossed in an image of Georgie as a CEO, put the handsome and happy husband at home in an apron, and felt much better about the whole thing. Well, not better, but more politically correct anyway. So long as it ended with Georgie in Hopeful—or Dallas or Austin, maybe— everything would come out right.

"I expect you're thinking about my family again," she said from behind him.

He turned and leaned back against the counter, watching her eat. Her hair was piled on her head, exposing the slender column of her neck. Her creamy skin had marks that he'd put there, and it filled him with a male satisfaction that was hard to deny. They weren't dark marks, or even very noticeable. But he knew.

"Hard not to. Rick asked me to check on you, not take you to bed and do dirty things to you."

She grinned. "And how I loved those dirty things. You can be dirty with me anytime, handsome."

Sam shook his head, though his heart rate kicked up just a bit. "What would your mother say if she heard you talk like that?"

"Mother believes that a woman should know her mind—and demand what she wants out of life."

"Somehow I doubt that extends to hot sweaty sex with tattooed soldiers."

She lifted an eyebrow. "And how would you know? For all we are aware, she loves hot sweaty sex. And tattooed soldiers."

Sam shook his head. "Do not put that image in my mind. Your mother is a fricking goddess who wears pearls to breakfast and gloves to garden parties."

Georgie was laughing. "Trust me, I could barely say it. But it was funny."

He couldn't help but grin too. "Fine, we'll leave it at that. But what do you want out of life, Georgie? Because your family seems to think you're up here brooding about your divorce."

"I am not brooding." She lay her fork down on the edge of the plate. "I like it here. Or I did until yesterday. But I like what I do, and I really like what we did last night. I'd like more of that. For right now, that's what I want."

He was all about more of last night. He shouldn't be, but he was. And he was damn glad to hear she wanted it too. But he had to be honest with her.

"You have to know that what we did last night was pretty spectacular to me too. It felt great, and I want more of the same. But, Georgie, we can't do this if you're thinking there's more to it than sex."

Because he had to be honest, even if it cost him another night in her arms.

She rolled her eyes. "Oh for God's sake. I should

have never told you I would have married you if you'd asked me twelve years ago. That was a fantasy, born of my youthful naiveté. I'm not that young or idealistic anymore. I'm capable of meaningless sex, Sam."

Meaningless? Why didn't he like that word?

"That's good to know. Because I have a crazy job, G. I can be here one minute and gone the next, and no idea when I'll be back again. You don't want to be a part of that."

"I'll decide what I want to be a part of, thanks." She picked up the fork again and finished the last bite of eggs. "But don't worry that I'm trying to turn last night into happily ever after. I had my taste of that fantasy, with the big wedding and the *till death do us part* bit, and I know it doesn't work out."

For some reason, it saddened him to hear her say that. Georgie was supposed to be the optimistic one. But she'd been burned, and it couldn't help but affect her.

Her phone rang then and she picked it up to glance at the screen. Then she groaned. "It's Rick," she said, looking up at him.

Sam felt a pinch in his chest. Maybe he shouldn't, but he did.

"Hey," she said, answering the phone brightly. Sam couldn't stay and listen to her talk to her brother, so he grabbed his own phone and went outside on the back deck. The day was still early and the sun sparkled on the water. A blue heron stood in the shallows, one foot raised, so still it looked like a statue.

Sam dialed HOT. Kev MacDonald answered. "Hey, Knight Rider. Just planning to call you."

His heart thumped. "Yeah? Got anything?"

"Kid's pulled up some video surveillance from the Metro. We'd like to have Dr. Hayes have a look. There's video of someone talking to Hamilton, but it's grainy. There's another shot, far better, of a face that looks like the man she described. But we need to be sure."

"All right. Want me to bring her there?"

"That's a negative. Richie's bringing it out."

It took Sam a moment to recall that Richie Rich was Matt Girard's team name. So far, he'd been thinking of him as Captain Girard. In the regular Army, even in a Special Forces battalion like the Rangers, officers were a separate species that did not mix easily with the grunts. But HOT had a different structure, and team camaraderie was critical. While it was appropriate to *yessir* the officers all day long, it wasn't inappropriate to refer to them by team names either. Matt Girard actively encouraged that kind of relationship with his team, but it would still take Sam some time to get used to thinking of his CO that way.

"We'll be here. I think shuffleboard starts in an hour, so maybe in between activities we'll find some time for videos."

Kev laughed. "Damn, man, you're gonna fit in here just fine. Call if you need anything."

"Copy," Sam said, smiling in spite of himself. He liked these guys a lot. He only hoped they were as good as they were supposed to be. If not, Georgie's life was forfeit. And that was something he couldn't let happen. With everything he had in him, he would fight for her, even if he had to risk his own life in the process.

He glanced into the house and saw her holding her cat and talking to it. He started to go back inside, but his phone rang again. Sam bit back a groan at the name on his screen. He had no choice but to answer.

When Sam came back inside, his expression was quietly grim. Georgeanne's heart turned over.

"What's happened?"

He only stared at her. "Rick just called."

Georgeanne sighed. Dammit. "Rick needs to mind his own business."

Sam scraped a hand over his head. "You told him you'd found a boyfriend and he could stop worrying about you. That you were having the best sex of your life and Tim was a pimple on the ass of life."

Georgeanne only felt a mild sense of embarrassment at having her words repeated back to her. She stroked Belle's soft fur and sighed. "I didn't want him to worry. And the sex was pretty good, but don't let it go to your head that I said that. It was a slight exaggeration for effect."

He looked murderous. "Jesus, Georgie. You just don't get it, do you? Your family is convinced you're a princess and only the best will do. Not only that, but they're also worried about their princess and this new man in her life when the old one was clearly so bad for her."

Annoyance flared inside her. "Why do you care? I didn't say a word about you." She spread her hand to encompass the cottage. "Or about this. I said I met someone and the sex was great. I wanted Rick to get off my back, okay?"

"Yeah, but guess who wants me to check out this new boyfriend of yours?"

Georgeanne rolled her neck to pop out the kinks. "So check him out and give Rick a glowing report. What's the problem?"

Sam stood there with his fists clutched at his side, his naked chest rippling with tattooed muscle, and a fierce expression on his face. Her core flooded with heat. Oh wow.

"The problem is that I have to lie. I'm expected to investigate the guy you're sleeping with, who just so happens to be me."

Georgeanne stood and walked over to him. She tilted her head back to meet his dark, glittering gaze. And then she put her hand on his pectoral, smoothing it down his abdomen and over the ridges of hard muscle. Her core was already wet.

"You aren't Rick's lackey, Sam. You have a job to do. Tell him you don't have time and tell him I'm a grown woman. It's as simple as that."

"Simple?"

She was gratified to hear his voice had dropped a few notches. Oh how she felt those sensual tones deep in the heart of her.

"I'm not wearing any panties," she whispered. "Doesn't that make it all better?"

"Georgie," he groaned. "You're killing me here."

She reached for his belt buckle. "Oooh, you feel that? The wind is blowing. Blowing my dress right off. Blowing you right where I want you."

For a minute, she thought he was going to resist her,

thought he would set her away and lecture her about her choices. But he didn't. Instead, he gathered her dress in his fists and lifted it over her head.

"You really aren't wearing panties."

"Of course not. I wanted to be ready."

He frowned as his fingers lightly touched the bruised skin of her hip. "I'd like to maim whoever did this to you."

"Forget about them. Take care of me. I need you. Can't you tell?"

He caressed her hot, wet mound, and she thrilled at the sound of satisfaction he made as her skin burned where he touched. She gasped when a finger ghosted over her clit.

"You're naughty, G. I had no idea."

She laughed softly. "I know you won't believe this, Sam—but I didn't know it either." She looped her arms around his neck and pulled herself closer to him. "You make me that way."

His teeth flashed white in his handsome face. "You're a pretty hot mess yourself, you know that? And I fucking love it."

He captured her lips, kissing her so deeply and passionately that she melted against him, clinging to him like she had not one ounce of strength left in her body.

His hands roamed over her, grabbed her ass and lifted her up so her head was higher than his. She tried to put her legs around him, but he stopped her, held her high with his arms wrapped beneath her bottom. He carried her like that to the nearest surface—the couch—and then sat her on the back of it. She opened her legs as he dropped to his knees in front of her.

And then he spread her open with his fingers and

curled his tongue around her clit until her nipples were tight, aching points and her body was on the edge of explosion. But he didn't let her finish that way.

Instead, when she was right there, right on the edge of bliss, he stood.

"Sam, I'm going to kill you," she gasped.

He unzipped his jeans and freed his cock. "Yeah, no doubt about it, babe. You're already killing me."

He was so hard and beautiful that she wanted to take him in her mouth and feel him pulsing against her tongue. Instead, he sheathed himself in a condom he produced from somewhere—and then he plunged inside her.

Georgeanne flew apart instantly, her body rippling with her orgasm, a raw scream issuing from her throat as Sam pumped into her harder, drawing out her release in ways she'd never known were possible.

How did he do this to her body? How did he know right where to touch her? How did he know what she needed before she did?

With Tim, sex had been good—sometimes even spectacular. But it did not feel like this—like her entire body was on fire with sensation, like she would die if she didn't have him inside her, stroking hard into her.

She didn't need Tim like she needed her next breath.

But she did need Sam that way. *Oh God.*

She tried to reason with herself. How could she need him when he'd only just come into her life again? How could she possibly think she needed him? She needed *this*. This thing he did to her. She did not need *him*.

This kind of thing was possible with another lover. Of course it was. Surely she'd had it with Tim too and she just couldn't remember it.

And yet, as Sam lifted her legs and wrapped them around his torso, she shuddered with the thought of any other man doing this to her. It *wasn't* possible.

Because there was no other man in the world for her but this one.

EIGHT

"IS THIS THE GUY?" MATT Girard sat at the small table in the kitchen and slid an 8x10 picture toward Georgie. Sam watched her reach for it with trembling fingers, and a wave of protectiveness washed through him. It was so strong he wanted to wrap her up in his embrace and never let her go.

She'd twisted him up inside but good. It was only a couple of hours ago that he'd been standing between her legs, buried deep inside her, the top of his head ready to come right off it felt so damn good. He wanted that again.

And then he wanted her to go back to Texas. He wanted her where she belonged, safe with her family, and he wanted her to find another guy to drive crazy with her hot body and wicked tongue.

He wanted a clear conscience again, but he knew he wasn't going to get it anytime soon. Yeah, he didn't really have to tell Rick anything—but he hated lying to his best friend. Rick only wanted what was best for Georgie, and while he knew she was an adult, he'd sounded pretty damn suspicious about the new man in her life.

"I don't want her hurt, Sam. Just check this guy out if you can, okay? Put the fear of God in him, same as always."

Same as always. Yeah, they'd been hell on the guys Georgie had started to "date" when she was fourteen. Oh, she hadn't been allowed to go on actual dates that early, but there'd been mall meets and football games and picnics where she'd pair off with some teenaged Lothario. And Rick and Sam were right there, frowning and wagging hypocritical fingers since they were also doing their damnedest to corrupt the teenage daughters of Hopeful's citizenry.

"That's him," Georgie said. She glanced up at Sam. He wanted to reach for her, but he didn't. Matt Girard's gaze bounced between the two of them for a moment. The dude wasn't stupid and there were definitely undercurrents in the room.

"All right. That helps. Thanks, Dr. Hayes."

He started to stand, but Georgie reached out and caught his arm. "I want to know what this is about."

She sounded fierce now, and Sam felt a swell of pride. And annoyance, since the less she knew, the better.

Matt glanced at Sam as he sat back down. Georgie withdrew her hand and tucked it into her lap.

"I can't tell you much," he began. "But this guy is known to associate with certain... elements, shall we say... that are wanted by the US Government."

"And this is why the military is involved instead of the cops?"

"Yes."

"Can you catch him?"

"We intend to. He hasn't left the country, so we'll get

him."

"I don't know who *we* are. How do I know you can manage this at all?"

Matt grinned. "We specialize in this kind of thing, Dr. Hayes. And though I can't tell you specifically who *we* are, believe me when I tell you this is all part of the daily routine for us. We'll get him."

Georgie looked annoyed. "Fine. But don't we have watch lists? How did this guy get into the US anyway?"

"He's a citizen. And yes, we have watch lists, and sometimes we… just watch."

"Watching didn't help Jake Hamilton a bit." Her tone was sharp and Sam winced. Just what he needed—Georgie pissing off his CO.

Matt Girard's gray eyes snapped with meaning. "Sergeant Hamilton had a choice. He made the wrong one."

Georgie seemed to deflate a little then. "I know that, but I'm still sorry it cost him his life."

Matt reached over and squeezed her shoulder, and Sam wanted to stop him from touching her for even a second. Jesus, what was wrong with him?

"I've been doing this job a long time, and I can tell you that it never gets easier to accept death. You get immune to it in some ways, but even that comes with a price. I'm sorry it cost him his life too, even if I'm not surprised."

Georgie bowed her head. "So what now? How long do I have to stay here?"

Sam tried not to read more into that question than necessary. It was normal she'd want to go back to her life.

"I'm afraid we don't know. But you're in good hands with Sergeant McKnight, so don't worry."

Matt stood then and Georgie brought her knees up, hugged them while she turned to look outside. Her cat jumped up on the table and head-butted her. She scratched the cat absently.

"McKnight." Matt jerked his head toward the door and Sam went with him. They walked outside and into the front yard. There was a driveway lined with trees that led out to a road about half a mile away. They were definitely remote.

Matt turned. "It's not my place to tell you how to conduct your personal affairs, but try not to let the lovely charms of Dr. Hayes cloud your judgment, okay?"

Sam stiffened. "Keeping her safe is my priority. It always has been."

Matt studied him. "Yeah, I can see that, *mon ami*," he said, his Cajun accent coming out like it did every so often. He took a piece of paper out of his pocket and handed it to Sam. "When I give you the signal, gonna need the professor to make a call."

Fear welled up hot and fast. "I can't put her in danger."

"We'll be here, Sam. HOT won't let anything happen to her. But we need these guys to come after her. The script is there, so get her to practice it, yeah? Once I give the signal, have her make the call. Those guys will come, and we'll scoop them up."

Sam's heart was pounding. "How can you be sure? What if they don't come? What if they decide to lie in wait somewhere for her?"

"They're desperate. Hamilton only gave them partial information, and they need the rest of it. We've been listening to the chatter, and Ibn-Rashad is getting pretty nasty. If they think Dr. Hayes has what they need, they'll come for her. We'll be here when they do."

Sam put the paper in his jeans pocket. How the fuck was he supposed to put Georgie in danger when he'd promised he never would?

Matt's expression was both sympathetic and determined. "I know what you're feeling. That sense of helplessness while you watch the woman you love do something insanely risky—but you have to trust it will be okay. She's strong enough to do this. And you're strong enough to stand there when she does. Evie proves it to me every day, believe me. Sometimes, all you can do is hold on for the ride."

Sam had heard about Matt's adventure down in Louisiana. There'd been organized crime, car chases, explosions, and a missing teenager, among other things. And though he'd gone down there single, he'd come back with a sexy chef who now wore a pretty spectacular engagement ring. Sam had met her once, and while she was smoking hot, what he really adored was the food she regularly sent into HOT HQ with Matt. Damn, that girl could cook.

Matt turned and got into his car while Sam stood there, hands shoved in pockets, and brooded. He couldn't stop thinking about one word his CO had used: love. What the fuck was that supposed to mean?

Of course he loved Georgie. He'd loved her since they were kids. But it wasn't *that* kind of love. How could it be? They'd only started having sex last night. Before that, they hadn't seen each other in six years. How on earth could romantic love be a part of the equation? And how could someone who didn't know either one of them all that well think it was?

Sam went back into the house after Matt's car disappeared from sight and found Georgie in the same position as when he'd left. Her eyes, when she turned to look at him, were troubled.

"This isn't going to end easily, is it?"

He wasn't sure what she was talking about. The situation with the Freedom Force—God, that was a fucking joke of a name, wasn't it?—or this thing between them. That's how twisted up she had him: he didn't even know what they were talking about.

She put her knees down and ran her hands through her gorgeous mane of hair—which had been hanging free since he'd unclipped it earlier. "Fucking terrorist assholes," she spat. "And fucking Jake Hamilton for being greedy or idealistic or whatever in the fuck he was being. He was an overachiever, and he liked nothing more than to get a perfect score. Bet it was the same thing with this DARPA shit. He wanted to do it because he liked the game, nothing else."

"I'm sorry, G. I know you liked him."

"I did. And I'm fucking pissed he did something so stupid."

"Some people are impatient. Or they don't think they're capable of getting what they want the regular way. Who knows what kind of background he had? He might have been poor or abused or any number of things that made him long to be something better in life."

Her eyes glittered with tears. "You were poor. Your parents mentally abused you. And the last thing you would ever do is try to sell government secrets to terrorists."

His heart flipped. "That's true. On all accounts." He

didn't like admitting what his childhood had been like, but Georgie already knew. She was one of the few who did.

She looked fierce all of a sudden. "You're a good guy, Sam. An amazing guy. I want to see you after this, and I don't care if my family knows. You make me feel good about myself. Not that I don't generally feel good or anything, but getting dumped knocked the wind out of me for a while. You make me remember what I felt like before any of that happened."

He swallowed hard. "That might be the nicest thing anyone's ever said to me. But you know it can't last, G. We're too different. I don't fit into your world—"

She swore so colorfully that he lost his train of thought. "What world? The one where I take the Metro to the Pentagon and teach college classes to military students? Or the one where all I can think about is having you inside me? Or maybe the one where I go to bed every night with a book and Belle and feel sorry for myself because my husband didn't find me interesting enough in the long run?"

"I already told you Tim was a fucking asshole," he growled. "But dammit, you know what I mean. You're Junior League, country club, everything I'm not. Hell, I don't even know the right word half the time and you teach the right words on a daily basis. I can conjugate fuck pretty well—but that's about it. I'm a soldier, Georgie. It's as simple as that."

Her eyes glittered. "I don't care, Sam. That's the part you don't get. I don't *care* what you think your place in my life is. I know where I want you, and you won't convince me otherwise." She pointed a finger at him. "And FYI, genius, but being a soldier is pretty damned awesome. Anyone who doesn't respect your accomplishments is stupid and not worthy of your time."

Now he was pissed. Because she wasn't listening and there was no way she was truly prepared for what life with him entailed. "Do you really want to be a part of this kind of life? The kind where I disappear for weeks on end? Where I can't call you and can't let you know that I'm even alive?"

She swallowed but didn't say anything, and he knew he'd made a point she couldn't refute. But he still kept going.

"Christ, Georgie, you freaked out because a student went missing from your class. What the hell will you do when it's me who's missing? Call my fucking boss and demand to know where I am? Do you really think that'll work?"

Her eyes filled with tears and his heart ripped in two. He didn't stay to see if they would fall.

Georgeanne watched Sam walk out of the house and into the yard. She wanted to call him back, wanted to say she was sorry, but he'd pretty much stunned her. And he was right. How could she stomach the life he led after she'd felt so out of control of her own life these past couple of years?

Tim had abandoned her for another woman. Jake Hamilton skipped class a few times and she'd gone looking for him. What would she do when it was Sam who left? How could she possibly have a life with him when he was right that she wouldn't like it?

And why did she even think she wanted that life? She'd had a crush on him once and they'd had sex. So what? That wasn't a recipe for the future, no matter that he made her feel good about herself again for the first time in a long time.

Georgeanne swiped her fingers under her eyes and wiped the moisture on her clothing. And then she grabbed her computer and determined to get some work done. Eventually, Sam came back inside. She didn't know what to say, so she didn't say anything. He walked over to her side and thrust a piece of paper at her.

"What's this?"

Sam looked grim. "You're going to have to make a call later, Georgie. It's best if you practice it so you can sound natural."

She read over the words, her blood going cold. "I'm supposed to tell them I have the information. And that I'll sell it."

Sam shrugged. "Yeah."

She read the paper over a few times. "All right." Because she would do whatever it took to capture this man. He'd killed Jake, and he'd tried to kill her. Plus she figured that if the military was after him, he clearly wasn't a nice person.

"You need to read it aloud."

She looked up at him, the paper still clutched in her hand. "Is this the kind of thing you do all the time?"

Sam was standing over her, hands in pockets, frowning. He hadn't said a word about earlier, but they both knew it was still there between them. "It's part of it."

She shook her head, the enormity of what he did pressing into her brain. "When you left to join the Army, I don't think I pictured this. I pictured tanks and guns. And believe me, I didn't like the idea of that at all. But this seems more frightening somehow."

"That's what I've been trying to tell you." He sucked in a breath, blew it out again. "I did the other stuff for a while. This is something new, and yeah, it's dangerous. But it's important, Georgie. What we do—the guys I work with, me—keeps this country safe."

She'd always thought of the Army as dangerous and she'd hated that he might be in jeopardy. But *this*. God. This secret organization—because she had no doubt that's what this was—was simply another layer to an already risky career.

"Are you happy with your choices?"

His jaw flexed. "Yes." He let out a sigh then and sat down across from her. "This job is me. It's something I'm good at. If I'd stayed in Hopeful, I'd have never amounted to much. Even with your family's influence. I couldn't afford college, and without that, there were no jobs I'd ever grow with. I didn't want the mill, Georgie."

"You could have gotten student loans, could have worked for my dad—"

"No." His voice was a whip in the air between them. "That's what you don't understand. What none of you understand. I'm not helpless and I'm not a charity case. Besides, I like what I do. It makes me damn proud to say I rescue people and stop terrorists, because not everyone can do it. But I can, Georgie. Me, fucked up Sam McKnight."

Her heart filled. Sam was driven to succeed, and he'd

done it on his own terms. He was still doing it. How could she fault him for that? She'd left Hopeful too and she didn't much appreciate her family trying to pull her back. "I understand."

His eyes said he didn't believe it. "Do you? Or are you just saying that?"

"I'm trying." She reached for his hand and squeezed it. "Yes, I care about you, and yes, it worries me that you're in danger. I'd be worried if you were a policeman or a fireman too. And you aren't fucked up. Or at least no more than the rest of us are."

"It's nice of you to say that."

She laughed. It wanted to turn into a sob but she wouldn't let it. "I'm not being nice. Trust me, I know fucked up. Just because someone seems to have a perfect life on the outside doesn't mean they do. My husband cheated on me, lied to me, and left me for another woman. I'd say that's pretty fucked up."

Sam sighed and scrubbed a hand over his head. "Yeah, all right, you got me there. We can both be fucked up then." He nudged his chin at the paper in her hand. "Now how about you read that a few times and let's see how it sounds."

After Georgeanne practiced saying what she needed to tell Jake's murderer, and Sam seemed satisfied, they fell into silence. He left her and went out into the yard to engage in some kind of workout routine that left her breathless just to watch. He was wearing athletic shorts, nothing else, and breathing deeply while moving through a set of exercises that left his body dripping with sweat.

Georgeanne tried not to ache deep inside, but that was about as fruitless as trying to prevent a dog from eating a plate of bacon left on the floor. She worked a bit, grading the papers she had left, looking over the final exam one more time. It was two days before it had to be administered and she held out a crazy hope this might all be over by then and she'd go back to her usual routine.

Well, except for one thing. She still wanted Sam as a part of her routine. She didn't know how that would happen, especially since he'd pointed out the obvious conflict between his life and hers. Yes, she had freaked out when her student went missing. And yeah, she'd had half a marriage with Tim for the last couple of years and she wasn't precisely ready to engage in the kind of relationship with a man where she had no idea where he was or what he was doing.

How would she handle that?

She'd felt a vague uneasiness over Tim's late nights at work, but she'd told herself it was silly. He was working hard at a new job. Except it wasn't that at all. Because he'd been working hard all right, giving it to Lindsey until late and then coming home and showering before crashing into bed and starting the whole thing over again the next morning.

Georgeanne bit her lip. God what a fool she'd been. But they'd been arguing so much then and she'd really preferred the quiet time alone when he was supposedly working. When weeks passed without sex, she'd felt relief rather than worry. Just when she started to believe something was wrong, Tim would make love to her and they'd have a blissful few days before everything went sideways again.

She looked at Sam where he still worked out, his muscles bunching and flexing and glowing with sweat. Her core clenched tight. How could she want to leap into a relationship with a man who would give her even less stability than Tim had?

Because she was crazy, that was why. She shook her head and tried to concentrate on her computer. When she read the same sentence for the twentieth time, she snapped the computer shut and propped her chin in her hands so she could watch Sam.

Eventually, he came inside and she pretended to be busy while he went and took a shower. They didn't speak much for the rest of the afternoon. Georgeanne didn't know what to say to him, so she said nothing. Sam spent time cleaning his weapon and reporting in to his super-secret military organization every hour.

When dinnertime rolled around, they ate leftover pasta with wine. Sam even baked a chocolate cake in the microwave, which she found super impressive. She told him so and he grinned.

"Even I can read a cookbook, G."

She took another bite of the cake. It wasn't beautiful, but it sure was good. "Yeah, but you don't have a cookbook here. You've memorized this, and I'm impressed. I wouldn't begin to know how to do it."

He shrugged. "You'd learn if you wanted. I like chocolate cake. And it's easier to learn how to do it yourself than buy a slice in a coffee shop."

"I don't know. I'd think the coffee shop was easier."

The look he gave her was full of meaning. "When there *is* a coffee shop. Sometimes there isn't."

He meant when he was deployed somewhere. She finished the last bite of cake and sighed. "Well, good news for your team members then."

His grin was genuine. "Yeah, I get stuck cooking when we have facilities."

She blinked. "And what do you do when you don't?" She didn't imagine they had takeout in some of the places he went to.

"MREs."

"Oh yes, how could I forget those?" Meals Ready to Eat came in sealed pouches, packed about a million calories per meal, and had been known to cause some pretty desperate trips to the restroom when you weren't accustomed to eating them. Or so she'd been told.

"No one ever forgets MREs, believe me."

"So I've heard." She got up and collected his plate and took everything over to the sink. She washed the dishes quickly, then set them in the strainer to dry. When she turned around, Sam was watching her, his expression intense and heated. Her heart skipped a beat.

"If I could be with anyone, I'd pick you," he said.

She licked suddenly dry lips. "You can. All we have to do is try."

He shook his head and her heart fell. "I already know how it'll go. Tried it once before and it didn't work out."

She didn't know why it pierced her to think of Sam having a relationship with another woman. She'd been *married*, for goodness sake. But it did kick her right in the chest to think of him with anyone else. Geez.

"I'm sorry it didn't work out, Sam."

He shrugged. "It's fine. It happens."

"What if I wanted to try anyway?"

She could tell he'd stiffened where he sat. "Best not to go down that road, Georgie. I'd rather have this—these few memories of you—than know I wasn't what you wanted me to be."

She wanted to go over and shake him. "You keep saying that. But how do you know what I want you to be? What if I just want you to be yourself?"

He got to his feet and stretched and she knew he was through with this conversation. "I better check in with HQ now."

He turned to walk away, but she couldn't let him go so easily. "You know," she called, "I had the *right* man with the *right* connections—and a fat lot of good it did me. The only person who cares that you aren't part of the country club set is you, Sam."

He turned back to her, his eyes glittering. "Maybe so. But that still doesn't change the fact that what I do isn't normal. Or stable. Are you ready for that, Georgie? Can you honestly say you are?"

Her throat was tight. "I don't know. But I'd like the chance to figure it out."

He looked cool and remote, and she knew he wasn't even considering it. Then he shook his head. "I'm right, Georgie. About everything. You'll realize it eventually. And you'll be thankful you had a near miss."

She wanted to growl. "Don't tell me what I'm supposed to be feeling. I'll work that out for myself, thanks."

He only arched an eyebrow before he pulled his phone from his pocket and walked outside. She watched him go down into the yard, away from her, and start to talk to someone on the other end. She wanted to scream. Instead, she hugged her arms around herself and wished this nightmare would soon be over. If she were in her home, her bed, her life—well, maybe she wouldn't ache so much when Sam McKnight refused to consider any kind of future where she might fit in.

When it got late, Georgeanne went to get ready for bed. Sam didn't even look up when she left, and she wondered how this night would go compared to last night. When she finished her nightly routine and went back out to the kitchen to grab some water, Sam was on the cot, eyes closed, arms folded over his impressive chest.

It was precisely what she expected—and yet she fumed for several minutes before she went and climbed into bed alone. Georgeanne Hayes was not begging. She'd come perilously close to it earlier, when he'd told her there was no chance for them, but that was a line she wasn't going to cross—no matter how needy she felt or how much she ached for him.

But of course sleep wouldn't come as she lay there alone, knowing Sam was in the next room, knowing what kind of heat they'd already shared. She'd been in bed for an hour, maybe two, lying awake with the covers tossed back and her heart pounding in frustration, when her door opened. Sam came in on silent feet and then stripped before lowering himself onto the mattress.

She wanted desperately to turn into him, to roll her hips against his body and beg him for fulfillment—but she was angry and she couldn't do that without being weak. She didn't like being weak.

"What are you doing, Sam?" she demanded. "I

thought we were finished."

He rolled her beneath him in a single smooth move and she realized he was hard. Her core flooded with heat. She barely suppressed a whimper. She should tell him to go away, but there was no way in hell she was going to do it.

No way.

"We should be, but God knows I can't get a moment's rest with you in the next room. Not when I want you so bad." He flexed his hips and her body arched up off the bed, though she willed it not to.

"Sam. My God…" Her voice was choked with need.

"This is what life with me is like, Georgie. Nothing for days on end—and then there I am, in your bed, in your life, wanting you to drop everything and be with me. Because I've been out in the field and now I'm back and I need you."

Her breath was coming faster now. She could tell it tortured him to say these things, but she wanted to hear it. Wanted to understand. His life terrified her, but she needed him all the same. "I like being needed."

"And if I only need you for sex? If all I want is a hot fuck before I'm gone again?"

"Maybe that's all *I* want. Did you ever consider that?"

He stiffened and she knew that thought had never crossed his mind. Well, hell, it hadn't crossed hers either, but damn if she'd let him be the one to say those kinds of things, to make assumptions about her feelings—even if they were mostly true.

She'd always done what she'd been expected to do. She'd married the proper guy and followed him around while he advanced in his career—and look how that worked out for her. Maybe it was time she did something shocking. Maybe it was time she threw herself into a sexual relationship with a man and worked out the details as they happened.

Except, God, she really didn't see herself operating that way. Not when the man was Sam and she'd loved him for half her life.

His mouth dropped to the column of her throat, and she sighed as his lips and tongue left a trail of flame in their wake. There was *nothing* better than this feeling she got when he was making love to her. Sam McKnight was her drug of choice, and she needed her fix.

Regardless that the fall to the bottom of the pit would be damn hard when it came.

"Georgie, you have to start thinking about this. You can't want me beyond these few days. I'm good for nothing but this kind of thing. I can't give you what you deserve."

She lifted her head and nipped his earlobe. "I'll be the judge of what I deserve." She wrapped her legs around his waist, held on tight. "Go ahead, Sam. Do what you think is your absolute worst. I need it. I need *you*."

He rocked into her body with a single sharp thrust and she gasped with the intensity of the pleasure he gave her. Everything felt so right when she was with Sam. So gloriously good.

He began to thrust into her hard, deep, and sure, until she was a mass of raw nerve endings, until the explosion took hold of her and magnified her senses to a keen edge. He followed her, her name a broken groan on his lips. And then he gathered her close and she remembered nothing else as she fell into a deep sleep.

Georgeanne wasn't quite sure, but she thought that Sam decided to stop fighting with her about the future. Or, at least, that he'd determined not to think about it. Because for the next two days, he was with her every moment. They spent hours in bed together, learning the taste and texture of each other, and they spent hours talking. About anything and everything—except for the specifics of his job in the military. She understood that part was off-limits, and she understood why.

But they did talk about the things he'd done, the places he'd gone. She learned the number and position of his scars, his callouses, the first time he'd shot a man, and the first time he'd been shot.

She ached for him, and she wanted to hold him tight and never let him go. Not that he would let her. If he had any idea how protective she felt, how angry she grew when she thought of him wounded and laid up in a hospital with no one to visit except his Army buddies, then perhaps he wouldn't tell her these things.

And that she could not bear. So she kept silent and she listened. And then she told him things about herself.

Sam wanted to know about her relationship with Tim, and she found herself saying things she never had to anyone else. Sam listened attentively, but he frowned a lot.

"He didn't deserve you, Georgie," he finally said.

Georgeanne felt a flood of warmth deep inside. "I know." And then she reached for his hand. "I know exactly what I deserve now."

He'd stopped protesting when she said things like that, but she didn't kid herself he'd made his peace with it. He still watched her with those wary eyes when he thought she didn't know it. She knew he was turning it over in his head, thinking about his job, about Rick and her parents, and about everything he thought he couldn't give her.

Of course she knew what her family wanted for her. They'd always wanted her coddled and privileged, wanted her to be with a man who didn't want her for the money in her trust fund.

Sam didn't want her trust fund, but he was certain her family would think he did. And he was too proud to endure that. She knew he didn't want handouts. From anyone. It tortured him to think her family might think less of him. She understood now that a great part of why he'd worked so hard to make something of himself was to prove that he could. To prove that her parents' faith in him hadn't been misplaced.

It touched her and broke her heart all at once. And she couldn't convince him it didn't matter because to him it did.

His phone rang on the fourth morning of their seclusion and they looked at each other for a long moment. Her heart thudded every time it happened, but so far it hadn't been the call he'd been waiting for. This time, however, he looked so solemn as he answered that she knew it was time.

And she knew what she had to say, knew what was expected of her. She was ready for it.

Sam's eyebrows climbed his forehead. "Really? Holy fuck... Just like that, huh? ... Lucky break... Yeah, yeah...

She's fine… Yeah… Copy."

When he ended the call, he just sat there for a second, staring at her. And then he reached over and hauled her into his arms. "It's over, Georgie. You're safe."

She wrapped her arms around him and held on tight. "How? Are you certain?"

"Yeah. They were operating out of a house in Greenbelt that the FBI had under surveillance. There's a witness who saw Hamilton there a couple of times. And we found video of the guy you saw, Abdullah al Fahd, close to the spot where Hamilton's body was found. The time stamp puts him there around the time of death."

Her heart hammered hard. It didn't seem real after the last few days of isolation and fear and preparation. "Is that enough? Will they be able to keep him over something like that?"

"There's more to it than that, but yeah, he'll go down for Hamilton's death."

"And the other guy? The one who threatened me in the coffee shop?"

His mouth tightened for a moment. "Gone. He was onboard a United Airlines flight to Cairo two days ago."

Georgeanne lay her head against Sam's shoulder and breathed a shaky sigh. "It didn't end quite the way I expected it to."

He squeezed her. "No, it ended far better. Sometimes it does, when things work the way they're supposed to. The cell was under surveillance and they made a mistake. Good for us, bad for them."

She leaned back and ran her fingers over his jaw. His eyes softened and her heart turned over as tenderness flooded her. She was glad it was over—and sad too, because once they were no longer forced to spend time in a confined little cottage, Sam would probably find it easy to avoid her.

"I want you," she said softly. "So much."

He turned his head and kissed her palm. "I want you too, Georgeanne. But there's no time."

She blinked. "No time?"

"Someone's coming to take you home." He stood and put her on her feet while she could only gape at him, her world crumpling in on itself in ways she hadn't expected.

"Why aren't *you* taking me?"

He looked solemn. "Duty calls, babe. I have a plane to catch and a war to fight. I don't know when I'll be back."

"Wow." Hurt swirled inside her, filling her with pain. She wanted more, and he wasn't going to give it to her. He really wasn't. And this was it. The end. He was going to use this as a reason to cut himself off from her. She knew it simply by looking at his face. "So this is how it ends, then? So long, thanks for the sex, and maybe I'll see you?"

"I told you this would happen. This is my life, Georgie."

He had told her, but she hadn't thought he meant he'd have to leave *right fucking now*. She hadn't been prepared for that. In the distance, she could hear a sound she hadn't heard the whole time they'd been out here in the Maryland backwater. Something large and mechanical was coming toward them—and then she realized what it was. The *whop-whop-whop* of a helicopter's rotors beating the air.

"There's nowhere for that thing to land," she said. It was the first thing to pop out of her mouth, and the farthest thing from what she wanted to say.

Sam, I love you. Come back to me. I need you.

"Nope," he told her. He went over and hefted the giant pack he'd left sitting in the corner the entire time they'd been here. And then he walked outside and waited while the helicopter got closer and closer.

"This is it? No goodbye?" Her eyes filled with angry tears and she berated herself for sounding so damn needy and upset. But her world was tipping on its axis and she was losing her footing.

His dark eyes raked over her. "I've been saying goodbye to you for two days, Georgie-girl."

She folded her arms over her breasts. "Yeah, but *I* didn't know it."

He snaked one arm around her and tugged her close. Then he lowered his head and kissed her, his tongue sweeping into her mouth and making her ache with need and want and sadness.

"Goodbye, Georgeanne. Take care of yourself."

"You'll be back, Sam. It's not like you're leaving forever." She knew it logically, yet it still made her panicky the way he was talking.

"I'm not leaving forever. And I *will* see you again. But maybe you'll have realized by then that it's never going to work between us." He grinned at her with that sexy smile of his. "It was fun, G. You're pretty spectacular— and Tim's a douche."

Her heart hammered as desperation and fear seeped into her. "You better come back and see me. I mean it."

He kissed her again, swiftly, then let her go and went out onto the driveway. The helicopter swooped in, the trees and grass blowing and twisting in the wind. Georgeanne put a hand on the railing and held on, though she was in no danger of blowing away. She felt like it though. Felt as light and insignificant as dandelion fluff.

A line dropped from the craft and a man rappelled down it. Then a ladder appeared and Sam stepped on. The helicopter started to rise even as he climbed. As she watched, a hand came out and tugged him into the open door.

And then the helicopter banked and zoomed out of sight.

Her heart hurt. Just hurt. Sam McKnight was gone and she had no idea when she'd see him again. Or even *if* she would. She had no clue what Sam was thinking. No freaking clue. What if he put in for a transfer or something? Or just never came to see her once he returned?

"Dr. Hayes?"

She blinked at the man standing on the lawn in front of her where Sam had so recently stood.

"Yes?"

"Soon as you're ready, ma'am, I'll drive you back to DC."

NINE

"WHAT THE HELL HAPPENED, GEORGIE? First there was a guy and now there's no guy." Rick sounded exasperated with her. And more than a little worried.

Georgeanne sighed and shoved her hair back from her face.

"I made him up so you'd stop bothering me."

Of course it wasn't true, but she wasn't telling her brother about Sam. Or about the blissful few days she'd spent wrapped in his arms in a cottage in Maryland.

Her heart ached every time she thought of Sam. She hadn't seen him or heard from him since he'd climbed into a helicopter three weeks ago and left her standing on the front step alone. He hadn't been kidding when he'd said his life was unpredictable.

Rick sighed. "Mother worries about you. I'm just trying to make sure you're all right since she won't ask you herself."

"She won't ask because she knows I'm a grown woman and I can take care of myself." Georgeanne tapped her pencil against the desk in her home office. "Rick, honestly, I'm happy with what I'm doing. I love my house, I love my job, and I'm not ready to jump into a relationship with anyone. And while we're at it, I don't appreciate you asking Sam to check on me. He has an important job and he doesn't have time to chase me down just because you ask him to."

"You're right," he said on another sigh. "I shouldn't have asked him. I tried calling him recently, but he must be out of the country again."

"He said something about going on a mission. I don't know where."

"How'd he look? Did he seem all right?" She could hear the concern in her brother's voice and it softened her attitude just a bit. Rick was a worrier by nature. When he loved someone, he was always concerned about how they were feeling. It was sweet, especially considering how tough her brother was in other ways.

"He seemed fine. It was good to see him."

"You still got a crush on him?" She could hear the laughter in his voice, but it was no laughing matter to her.

"And what if I did? Would you freak out if I went out with him?"

She could almost see Rick's face. He'd be blinking right about now. Processing what she'd said. "It would be a little weird for me, sure. He's my best friend and you're my sister. But I suppose I'd get used to it. Why? Is there something you aren't telling me?"

"Not at all. I just like yanking your chain." Because some things were private. Not only that, but her brief affair with Sam McKnight seemed to be over and done. There was nothing to tell.

They talked for a few more minutes—about Hopeful,

116

about their mother's upcoming garden party, about their father's golf trip, about Rick's wife and kids—and then hung up with a promise to speak again soon.

Georgeanne stared at the phone and heaved a sigh. Talking to Rick, hearing the laughter of his kids in the background, talking about their parents—everything about it made her feel her loneliness keenly. Some days, she thought returning to Hopeful was a good idea.

But she usually came to her senses before she put the house on the market and started to pack.

Georgeanne worked on the syllabus for her next class, which started on Monday, and then decided it was time for bed. She went up to her room, got undressed, and climbed under the covers with her book. Belle jumped on the bed and proceeded to take a bath.

"We lead an exciting life, don't we, Belle?"

The cat didn't answer, and Georgeanne gave up on her book and turned on the news. And then she must have dozed off because the ringing of her phone scared the hell out of her. She grabbed it from the bedside table. When Sam's name popped up on the screen, she nearly dropped the phone as she tried to slide the bar before it went to voice mail.

"Hello?"

There was silence on the other end and her heart fell. Dammit, she'd missed him. Would he leave a message? Did she even want him to? Or was it better if she just considered the time in the cottage to be the coda to their relationship?

"Hey there, G."

He sounded so good. Her shoulders sagged with relief—both that she'd caught the call in time and that he obviously wasn't dead.

"Hey, Sam. Long time, no hear."

He chuckled softly. "Yeah. I told you that could happen, didn't I?"

"You did. I just didn't realize you meant quite so literally or quickly." And she was still processing how she felt about it, especially since he was now calling her up out of the blue. It wasn't quite the same as her and Tim inhabiting different orbits while in the same house, but still.

"That's what life with me is like, babe. Here one day, gone the next. Radio silence for weeks. I tried to tell you."

"I know, and I appreciate it."

"Still think it's something you can handle?"

Georgeanne nibbled the inside of her lip. She'd been thinking about that a lot while he'd been gone. And though there was no easy answer, there was only one she could give. Because when it came right down to it, she needed him in her life. "I'll learn to handle it."

"Are you sure about that? Because it won't be easy, G."

She swallowed as tears welled behind her eyes. "I know. But you're worth it, Sam. You're worth it to me."

He didn't say anything and she strained to hear him, wondering if he'd hung up on her.

"You still there?"

"Yeah, I'm here."

She let out a shaky sigh. "So where are you now? Back in the CONUS?" She loved that she could use military lingo with him and know, at least a little bit, what she was talking about.

She thought he might be grinning. "I am."

"Which part of the CONUS?"

This time he laughed. "You like saying that, don't you?"

She smiled. "Who wouldn't? The military has such interesting terms for things, don't you think? CONUS for continental US. TDY. AWOL. Hoo-ah. It's fascinating."

"I didn't call you for a lesson on military acronyms, babe."

"No, I don't suppose you did." Her heart was filling with warmth as they talked. It was a strange conversation in some respects, but if he was calling, then he must care at least a little bit. "So where are you right now then?"

"Right now?"

"Right damn now."

"Standing on your front steps. Wondering if I should ring the bell or go."

Georgeanne gasped. And then she dropped the phone in her haste to get out of bed. "Don't you dare leave, Sam!" she yelled as she grappled for the phone.

She ran down the stairs and yanked open the front door. Sam stood there with his phone to his ear. He lowered his arm slowly. They stared at each other.

"Looking kinda sexy in my shirt, G," he said softly.

She crossed her arms self-consciously. She was wearing one of his T-shirts that he'd left in the cottage. It was not sexy. It swam on her. But it made her think of him, and so she wore it anyway even though she got hot in the middle of the night and had to sleep on top of the covers.

"I missed you," she said simply, her eyes welling with tears.

"I missed you too." He cocked his head to the side. "You still naked down there?"

"I'm wearing panties."

His teeth flashed white in the darkness. "I meant something else. Thought about that a lot out in the field this time. Damned embarrassing a couple of times, if you know what I mean."

"The fellas don't appreciate a good hard-on?" she teased, her heart racing a mile a minute.

"Oh, I think we all appreciate them. When they belong to us and there's a hot woman to appreciate it with us in private."

"I see."

He came the rest of the way up the steps, until he loomed over her. He was wearing desert camouflage BDUs and he looked utterly delicious.

"Gonna invite me in?"

"That depends."

He looked suddenly wary. "On what?"

Georgeanne held the door tightly, like she needed it to stand. Or maybe to keep from flinging herself in his arms before she had an answer. "On why you're here. Is it for a hot fuck? Or something else?"

Sam looked at her standing there in his T-shirt, her pretty green eyes fixed on his face, all the hurt and confusion she felt showing in them, and he wanted to drag her in his arms and just hold her tight.

Why was he here? Because he couldn't stop thinking about her. Because he'd left that cottage determined to make a clean break with her, and then he'd been haunted by memories of her out in the field. Oh, not when it counted. When it counted, he was able to blank his mind of everything but the job.

But when he wasn't humping through the desert or bursting into a compound to rescue frightened tourists who'd been taken hostage by yet another group with an axe to grind against Americans, he'd thought of Georgie and the way she'd made him feel.

Like he belonged. Like he was special. Like he'd come home.

But the words lodged in his throat. He was still too uncertain of himself, of what he felt, to try to give it a voice. Finally, he managed to speak. He hoped it was good enough.

"Because I need you. Because I missed you. Because, when I thought of everything I wanted to do when I got back, none of it meant a damn thing if you weren't a part of it."

She wrapped a hand in his shirt then and tugged him toward her. He entered the house, waited for her to shut the door and lock it. And then he pushed her back against the door and buried his face in her hair.

"Georgeanne. God, I missed you." She smelled so sweet, like flowers and cake, and he wanted to devour her.

Her arms looped around his neck. She splayed a hand over the back of his head. "Sam. Oh, Sam. Don't you leave me like that again."

There was a lump in his throat. "I already told you—"

"I know. You have to go when you have to go. But you don't have to go without telling me you want me again. You don't have to let me think you're finished with me. With us. Maybe I can handle you leaving if I know you still need me."

He nuzzled the side of her neck. "I'm not sure I'll ever be finished."

She squeezed him tight then. "I love you, Sam. I don't care if that makes you uncomfortable. I love you and I won't keep it a secret any longer. From anyone."

His heart had stopped beating in his chest. And then it lurched forward again, beating harder and faster than before. He straightened so he could see her eyes.

She bit her lip, that sweet plump lip that he wanted to nibble and suck. "I'm sorry if that bothers you," she said. "But I can't help it and I won't hide it. And if that makes you want to run away, then I guess I'll have to fight to keep you from doing it."

His throat ached. "Run away? Yeah, it kinda does. But it also makes me want to strip you naked and worship every inch of your body until I can't move anymore."

She feathered her fingers over his cheek. They were trembling. "You'll have to be a little plainer with me, Sam. Tell me what it means that you aren't running. Tell me what this is to you. What *I* am to you."

His heart hammered. "I can't forget you, Georgie. I can't quit you either. I've thought of you for twelve years, and once I had you—really had you—I knew I was in trouble. Because I don't care how pissed off Rick gets at me, or how disappointed your parents are because I'm not what they envisioned for their princess. I want you. I need you." He swallowed hard. Jesus, was he going to frigging pass out here? Why were the words so damn difficult to say? "You're everything to me," he finished, disappointed in himself for not being able to say the three words he should say.

He'd been thinking about them a lot over the past few weeks and he knew they were true. He didn't know when it had happened, or why he couldn't dig her out of his heart the way he wanted, but he'd given up trying. She was the one obstacle he couldn't defeat.

And maybe she wasn't an obstacle. Maybe she was the best damn thing to come into his life and he just had to figure out how to make it work. In any event, he wanted her in his life and he would fight to keep her there.

She smiled in spite of his lack of finesse with words. "You love me. I knew it." She gave him a smug look. "Bet you fell for me when I was following you around the house all those years ago. God knows I was pretty irresistible."

He laughed and ached all at once. "About as irresistible as a rash."

She pinched his arm and he laughed again. "You're a hot mess, Sam."

"You make me crazy, G." He ran his hands up her sides, under the T-shirt, and cupped her warm breasts in his palms.

"You make me crazy too, Sam. And I don't know how this is going to work out, and I can't guarantee I won't freak out when you're gone, but I love you and I want to try. I'm tired of playing it safe. If it doesn't work, then at least we'll know. But I want that chance. I need that chance."

He ran his thumbs over her nipples, thrilled to the catch of her breath in her throat. "I know. I need that chance too. I need you." He dipped his head and kissed her lightly, though she tried to deepen the kiss. He pulled back while she whimpered and squeezed her breasts lightly in his palms. "I've thought of little else but this for the last three weeks."

"You know what I thought about?"

He shook his head. She unbuckled his belt, unbuttoned his pants—and then her hands wrapped around his swollen cock. He didn't know what to expect—but she dropped to her knees and tilted her head back to look up at him.

"This," she said. "I thought about this."

And then she took him in her mouth and his knees nearly buckled.

"God. Georgie." He braced a hand against the wall and swallowed. Her tongue rolled over him, her fingers pumped him, and it would just be so frigging easy to let her get him off this way.

But it wasn't what he'd envisioned during the long, lonely stretches on watch. He reached for her, pulled her up and ripped the shirt she wore over her head at the same time. Then he filled his hands and mouth with her breasts. She clutched his shoulders, gasping, and he knew what an utterly perfect night he was in for.

But he suddenly didn't want it here, like this, in her hallway. Up against a wall. There was plenty of time for that kind of thing, but right now he wanted her beneath him in a bed. Wanted her legs around him and her mouth on his.

He swept an arm behind her legs and scooped her into his arms. And then he took the stairs two at a time. When he reached her room, the television was on and the cat was parked in the middle of the bed.

The cat took one look at the two of them and bolted.

Sam laid Georgie on the bed and stripped her panties off. Then he was between her legs, his pants shoved down his hips, rolling on a condom with shaking hands.

And then finally, finally, he was inside her. Loving her. Feeling the utter rightness of what she did to him. He loved her cries, loved her breathy moans. She shattered quickly, her body tightening around his, her inner muscles squeezing him hard, his name on her lips.

He followed her over the edge, a groan ripping from his throat. And then he held her, his heart beating hard, and knew he'd only ever felt this way with her. This exhilarating rush of emotions and sensations.

Sam propped himself up on an elbow, pushed the hair off Georgie's face, and smiled down at her. "I love you," he whispered, finally finding his voice for what he wanted to say. "I love you so much."

Her eyes glistened and she smiled that beautiful smile that he felt belonged to him alone.

"I know," she said. "And you have no idea how happy that makes me."

Warmth blossomed inside him. This felt so right. Here, with Georgie. His tormenter. His love. "I'll do the best I can to make you happy. Always."

"I know you will. I believe in you."

Her faith in him was a gift beyond measure. "You have no idea what it does to me to hear you say that."

She traced her fingers over his lips, softly, lightly. "You're mine now, Sam. I'm not letting you go. Ever."

"There's no one else I'd rather belong to." He tucked his head into her shoulder and breathed her in as belonging filled his soul. "*You* are my home, Georgie. Only you. Always you."

She punched him lightly on the arm. "Damn you," she whispered and he looked up to see tears sliding down her cheeks. "I didn't want to cry."

He grinned at her. "Who's the hot mess now, huh?"

"I blame you." She swiped the tears away and pushed at him until he rolled over. He was still half in and half out of his cammies. Her fingers went to the buttons of his shirt, flicking them free.

"You'll have to pay for making me cry," she said as she opened his shirt and pushed up the T-shirt beneath. Then she sat up and just stared at him before slowly shaking her head. "Wow, who knew a uniform, tattoos, and muscles could be so appealing?"

She picked up his dog tags where they lay against his skin, fingering the edges. Then she dropped them again and stretched out on top of him.

"What happened to making me pay?" he asked when she just lay there and hugged him.

"I'll get to that," she murmured against his skin. "Right now, I want this. Just you and me and our hearts beating together."

He slid his arms around her and squeezed. "That's what I want too. Forever."

THE END

Thank you for reading *Hot Mess*! I hope you enjoyed it. If so, please consider helping others to enjoy this book by:

Recommending it! Please help other readers find this book by recommending it to friends, readers' groups, and discussion boards.

Reviewing it! Please tell other readers why you liked this book by reviewing it at the retailer you purchased it from or at Goodreads.

Lending it! Where possible, this book is lending-enabled – please lend it to a friend!

Many thanks for all you do to help make this book a success!

The best way to keep up with the news from me, including when there will be more **Hostile Operations Team** books available, is to sign up for my spam-free newsletter here: http://eepurl.com/c5QFY

WHAT'S NEXT

More HOT guys, of course! If *Hot Mess* is your first taste of the HOT world, check out Book 1 in the Hostile Operations Team series, *Hot Pursuit.* Coming in November, watch for a HOT Christmas novella titled *Hot Package*! Sometime in the spring of 2014, look for *Dangerously Hot,* which is Book 2 in the HOT series. If you're counting, that's **four** stories (2 novels, 2 novellas) set in the HOT world that will be available within the next few months! Yippee!

ACKNOWLEDGMENTS

AS ALWAYS, THERE ARE MANY people to thank whenever a book goes out into the world. I'm so grateful to all of you, my readers, who have embraced the HOT world and asked me for more stories. I love writing military heroes and you've given me a reason to continue!

Once again, my husband Mike, an Air Force veteran and all around great guy, was invaluable with his encouragement and advice and military knowledge. Any mistakes are mine alone. One of the reasons I chose to create my own Special Operations team was so I could do whatever I wanted with them.

Thanks as always to Alicia Hunter Pace, aka Jean Hovey and Stephanie Jones, who have been there for many brainstorming sessions and tossed out some very valuable ideas. I think we've got HOT covered for a few more books now.

Without my fab editor Robin Harders, who knows where this story would be? Robin is responsible for telling it like it is when I try to cut corners. She makes me dig deeper and work harder and tries to gently point out my bad habits. I grumble and gripe, but I roll up my sleeves and do the work.

Anne and Sara at Victory Editing are amazing and I couldn't live without them! They make sure words are correctly used, punctuated, and make sense in context. (And if you find mistakes in this letter, it's because I didn't pass it through them first!)

I also have to thank Amy Atwell at Author E.M.S., who does the formatting of my books so that I can continue to write new stories. And Frauke Spanuth at Croco Designs has once more created the perfect cover. She also maintains my website, which is fortunate for me because it's always beautiful and frequently updated.

Finally, I want to thank the authors who've been so generous with sharing their knowledge as I embark on this indie journey. Courtney Milan, Marie Force, Melody Anne, Kathleen Brooks, Liliana Hart, Ruth Cardello, Sandra Marton – and so many more that to list them all would take pages!

Once more, thank you for reading and I hope you enjoy my HOT military guys!

ABOUT THE AUTHOR

USA Today bestselling author Lynn Raye Harris lives in Alabama with her handsome former-military husband and two crazy cats. Lynn has written over fifteen novels for Harlequin and been nominated for several awards, including the Romance Writers of America's Golden Heart award and the National Readers Choice award. Lynn loves hearing from her readers.

For more information on all of Lynn's books,
visit her at http://www.LynnRayeHarris.com/books

Connect with me online:
Facebook: https://www.facebook.com/AuthorLynnRayeHarris
Twitter: https://twitter.com/LynnRayeHarris
Website: http://www.LynnRayeHarris.com

Made in the USA
Lexington, KY
07 March 2015